The author has lots of ideas for stories as this shows in his books. He could have two books he is writing at one time, his ideas come from his background of travelling around the world in his younger days, visiting other countries and learning their culture. He would like to live in Spain but his roots stop him as he loves the UK. He feels he could do a follow up book on Rubin.

I thank my wife and children who had the patience to listen to me while writing this book but seemed more concerned to see it in print and on the shelf.

JJ Jonson

RUBIN

AUSTIN MACAULEY PUBLISHERS™

LONDON · CAMBRIDGE · NEW YORK · SHARJAH

A CIP catalogue record for this title is available from the British Library.

ISBN 9781528945981 (Paperback)
ISBN 9781528971607 (ePub e-book)

www.austinmacauley.com

First Published (2020)
Austin Macauley Publishers Ltd
25 Canada Square
Canary Wharf
London
E14 5LQ

I am pleased that I could google the information I needed to get the information correct.

You know when you get up and you start to have one of those days when you know that if you do anything, it goes wrong? You spill your coffee, can't make a knot in your tie and you keep pulling it off. I don't know if I count to ten, it will work as I am so pissed off and my day has not even started yet. It's only 6:00 a.m. I have got to get to Heathrow airport and fly by 2:00 p.m. Luckily, I live near Northampton. Right, check I have everything packed in my briefcase. Then my phone rings. *You? What now? It's only 7:00 a.m.* I pick my phone up. It's Sonia, my girlfriend.

"How are you?" she says.

"Oh, why? I'm having a bad start to the day," I shout.

She says, "Calm down and concentrate."

"Okay, babe. I will call you when I land, love you."

Call finished. I should not have stayed at hers and left early at 3:00 a.m. this morning, but she loves me. Maybe I can rest on the plane. Now I get into the car with my suitcase and briefcase to go to Heathrow airport, start the car and then see that I need petrol. *You silly bastard*, I think, *you should have filled it up last night instead of going to Sonia's for a meal and drinks.*

Right, now I have filled it up and here we go. Time is ticking. I get to the airport around 11:30 a.m. so I have plenty of time. Thank God! Maybe my day will be okay from now on. I get to the check-in desk for British Airways. Lovely female on the desk. Can't help smiling at her. "Did you pack the case yourself?" she says.

"Yes, all by myself," I reply cheekily.

She looked up and smiled at me and said, "Have a good flight, Mr Johnson." The day is getting better I thought, so I checked in. Went to passport check and security. Now for a sandwich and a coffee that I won't spill this time. Phone rings.

"Good morning, Mr Johnson! How are you?" It's my PA, Lauren, very good at her job, sometimes too good.

"Okay," I say, "In the airport and checked in."

"That's great. Don't forget you will have somebody waiting for you, a driver to take you to your hotel in Domodedovo. That is where you are going when you land in Moscow."

"Yes. Thank you, Lauren, for getting it all in order."

"Okay," she says, "See you in a few days with plenty of orders."

"I will do my best. Bye."

I have never been here before and it's November, so it will be cold. I'm thinking if I have brought enough clothes.

Over the Tannoy comes the call to go to gate 13 and board this plane. *Unlucky gate number*, I thought. *Now that I am first class, I get more space and I can do some work on my laptop*, I thought to myself. As I was shown to my seat, I noticed a Latin American lady seated next to me. *Wow*. I thought what a looker and a body to die for. She looks at me, smiles and says, "Are you staying long in Moscow?"

"Only a few days. I have business meetings all the time that I will be there."

"Oh shame, all work and no play makes for a dull man. How boring! My name is Maria, we shall meet up some time and I will show you the night life in Moscow."

"Sounds good to me," I said "my name is Rubin."

"Hello Rubin," she said with a smile. "What hotel are you staying at?"

"I don't know until my driver picks me up and takes me to it; my PA booked it."

She seemed impressed, gave me a lovely smile and blew me a kiss. I am hot under the collar now. We take off and I open my laptop. I look over to her and she seems to be watching a film with her headphones on. I think no more of it until I look up and see her taking my picture on her phone, "Just so I know what you look like when we meet again." I think nothing of it. I get up to go to the loo, I notice that in front of me is a mean looking dude, huge body, the sort of a man you see at the Olympics. I go to the loo and then come back to my seat to find him looking straight at me so, I turn my head away. Then, I see Maria looking at me and smiling. So, the day might be okay after all.

I am checking the time zone in Russia for when I land. It has eleven time zones. Which one am I going to be in? So, I politely get Maria's attention. She takes her headphones off and looks at me startled. I say, "Sorry. I did not mean to shock you. I was wondering if you knew what time we land as I guess it's different to the UK."

She says, "It will be three hours ahead from now."

"Thank you." Then I work out I have lost six and a half hours with the flight time as well. We land and I find myself walking with Maria. We are just having a small talk on the way to the baggage reclaim area. I find my case, then I see her pick up a small case. It did not seem heavy. *She must travel light*, I thought. I come out of the terminal and see her talking to that big guy on the plane. She nodded to him and carried on. Must be her body guard. As I am coming out, I see a nice female with a board with my name on it. As I approach her, she says, "I am your driver."

My driver was in a smart uniform and did not speak the whole time on our way to the hotel. She stopped the car outside of this lovely hotel and I stepped out. She gets my case out, I take it from her and proceed to the desk where a man says, "Good day, Mr Johnson! I hope you had a good flight."

I say, "Yes. Thank you."

"Here is your room number 13."

God no, not thirteen again. I get into my room and it was unbelievable. Gold taps and a very large bath, big enough for two. Everywhere you looked round this room, it could not be faulted. Lovely, huge bed. *What a waste*, I thought. It was like three rooms. It was magnificent.

So, this time Lauren has done me proud. Maybe because I said the last hotel that she booked me was shit.

I cleaned up, went down for the dinner and got seated at the corner table. It's really good, as I can see the other guests and watch people who look like they have money. I don't know any Russian, so if anyone talks about me and looks at me, I will just smile back.

I think this wine is going to my head a bit, I seem to be smiling a lot. *Maybe not a bad day*, I thought.

Then it hit me how can Maria find me if she does not know where am I staying. Oh well, never mind. I go to my room. I had gone for about one hour so, I get back to my room feeling happy. When I open the door, I am in shock, as my room is in a mess. All my clothes are tipped out all over the bed. My laptop is still there and my phone is in my pocket so what were they looking for? Then my mobile rings. It's Sonia. "I just wanted to know how you are and if you are there."

We have a small talk about nothing really, then I say, "I love you." I say nothing about the room. "Bye." Really, I could do without her right now.

It has now got me thinking that someone is watching me or wants something from me. I run a large company with about 150 employees. We make spy cameras, parts for missiles, lots of components for rockets and we are developing some new ideas. I have meetings arranged for me to go to India, the USA and then China. It seems that my company is growing all the time.

I am getting tired so I pick the room phone up and I can hear people talking then a 'click' and a voice says, "Hello, Mr Johnson. How can I help?" I ask for a car for 9:30 in the morning and explain where I wish to go. "No problem. That is arranged for you. Anything else I can help with?" I say nothing about the room being ransacked. He probably knows.

"No, thank you."

I put the phone down and think I have a big meeting tomorrow with a major player in my market so I need to sell some of my products.

I did not sleep very well. Not that the bed wasn't comfy and all quiet, but I kept thinking about the number thirteen and my room number; it was disturbing. I went down for the breakfast. *Not many people here this morning. All having breakfast in their rooms maybe*, I thought. I order some coffee and scrambled eggs, with bacon and toast.

Then the waiter appears, "More coffee, sir?"

"Yes, please." It's not bad, this coffee. I do like it with the strong flavour. I am just about to leave when the waiter comes up.

"More coffee, sir?"

"No, thanks." Is he trying to keep me here or what? He keeps looking at me!

I enter my room with suspicion but I don't find anything out of the place this time. I get ready and make a quick call to Sonia. Then, before I go, I leave my spy pen in the room so it will contact my mobile if anyone enters this room.

I am waiting in the lobby when this smart lady comes over and says, "Your car is ready for you. This way." She goes first and opens the door for me to get in while I sit there and watch all the traffic. It is busy on these roads, reminds me of London's traffic. I take my laptop out of my briefcase and check what they are interested in.

It seems a long drive to this place and when we stop outside this huge building, it reminds me of a castle. It was stony pink in colour.

The driver opens my door. As I step out, I see two men standing at the door. As I walk towards them, one says, "Good morning, Mr Johnson," and opens the door. The other one says, "Follow me please." We walk into a large hall. It was all marble with huge paintings everywhere on the walls. Very impressive.

"Wait here, please." Then he leaves me standing there and I hear footsteps. A short man comes to me and says, "Would you come with me, please?" So, I follow him. We get into a lift and up three floors. The door opens and he says, "Please wait in that room. Your name is on the table."

"Thank you," I say and walk into this huge room with a very large oval table laid out with coffee, tea and juice. It had about eight seats round the table, I think I will have it tough here if all the seats get filled. Although it is freezing outside, it is too hot in here. What a heating bill they must have!

When I looked at the table, I saw my name on it. So, I stood near it and waited, thinking that I know how I want to impress the clients; I have done this sort of thing many times, but this seems to be different. This is the headquarter of a major company. I look at my watch and realise that I have not changed the time. Then a noise from the other side of the room made me look up. Door is opened by two men in suits and then three men appear, all different heights. It made me think of the three stooges (bit naughty, I know) all in smart suits, one with fair hair, and another man behind them. Tall, very smart, they walk to their seats then wait till this man sits down. Then we all sit down and he speaks looking at me and says, "I am the CEO of my company, the Heysel Group. We own several companies, so I welcome you, Mr Johnson, to our country. These other men are my technicians, who will guide me through your plans. May we look at them? Have some coffee." In my experience, it is difficult with a hot drink to sell, so I refused.

I get some plans out that I think they would be interested in and after a while they all look and nod to the CEO.

He starts with, "Well, Mr Johnson, it looks like we can do business."

I smile and say, "Thank you." I did leave some plans in my case as a backup. Time was ticking while I was explaining information about the things they were asking about.

The CEO says to me, "Come Mr Johnson, we will have lunch now."

So, I put all the papers back in my case and take it with me as men walk back through the doors that they came in. So, I follow and, to my surprise, there is a table laid out fit for a king. There are five seats. It has dainty cutlery and decorated plates and glasses. As I sit down, I notice that there are waiters standing all around the table, serving us food on our plates, whether you wanted or not. It was nice and tasted good. Two glasses of wine and I felt good. Then the CEO stands up and all the other men followed. I join them. He says, "Thank you,

Mr Johnson. I think we will do business and I look forward to seeing you at my factory tomorrow. My driver will pick you up at your hotel at 9:00 a.m. Is that good for you?"

"Yes sir."

"Leave your details with my men. Thank you and bye."

He leaves and the men follow; we have not finished our meals but he is – the Guv'nor.

I turn to leave with my briefcase and a man approached me, "Come this way, sir," and I follow him to the lift then down to the hallway. There a man on the door is waiting to see me out. My car is waiting and the driver opens my door. Off we go! I wish all meetings were like this one. The driver still says nothing on the way back to my hotel. It seems everything here works like clockwork. I am impressed. We then arrive, I get out of the car and go through the lobby.

As I walk through the lobby, I hear a voice saying, "Hello, Mr Johnson! How are you?" I turn around and it is Maria, looking like a million dollars. I am gob-smacked.

"Hi!" I say. "How are you?"

"Enough of the small talk. I have come to take you out for the night, see the sights and have a meal."

God, what a day! Am I dreaming? I need to pinch myself. This is me and I am not dreaming.

"I need to freshen up and get rid of my briefcase."

"You have fifteen minutes. Don't be long."

It was the quickest shower I had. I like long showers to unwind but can't keep a girl waiting, so change of clothes and smellies and I am done. I go down and she is waiting. She stands up and smiles again when she sees me and says, "Come on, my car is waiting." Can this day get any better?

We are sitting in the back of the car when she puts her hand on my knee. Now, I own a big company and I am a strong person, but this, and the smell of her perfume, it just was too much. I felt like jelly. "We will have a good evening, Rubin."

She turns and kisses me. I don't hold back. I embrace it for a long time, I can't resist her, I have a fantastic feeling and she kisses me again. I don't resist and kiss her back. I have a magical feeling running through my body and I see nothing but her when I close my eyes.

We stop outside this building with people waiting outside in a queue, three doormen outside the building look very impressive; it looks like you'll get in only if they say so. As we get out of the car Maria holds my hand. "Come on," she says. We go straight to the doormen, then I see Maria move aside and say hello to one of them. Later, he gestures us to go straight in; I think she has been here before. As we walk in, you can hear the music and see people dancing; lovely big bar and staff walking about, serving tables. But a member of the staff comes over to Maria and says, "Follow me, please."

She is still holding my hand and I feel like the cat who's got the cream. She leads me to another room set up with a table and chairs very sumptuous. We sit down and say, "Champagne, thank you."

I say, "This is a very nice place; you must know the owner."

She giggles and says, "Yes I do. It's me!" Now we eat lobster and other shellfish, all being washed down with champagne. We have lots to talk about, followed by dessert and then brandy.

"Would you like a cigar?" Maria says.

"No, thanks. I don't smoke."

"Good," she states firmly.

I don't like smoky breath. *God*, I'm thinking, *where's this leading to? I have a good idea!* She stands up smiling and says, "Come on. We will go back to your hotel for a nightcap." Not only is she good looking and a body to die for, she is very forward in her ways too. I noticed before we came in this room, she was looking around the night club, checking in her head that if it was running smoothly or not.

Next, we are walking through the dance area and out onto the street, into her waiting car and in the back seat where we cannot keep our hands off each other. Touching and kissing and laughing at each other. So, we are back at my hotel, straight off to my room and in we go.

We are standing up and kissing, then she pushes me onto the bed. She stands up and starts to take her dress off, she unzipped it at the back and it falls to the floor. I then see her body, she is naked, nothing on underneath the dress. What a shock! She just stands there and smiles at me. I get off the bed and start to undress. *God, why is it more difficult for a bloke to undress?* Now I am naked and I walk up to her and we wrap our arms round each other. She smelt lovely and the warmth of her body against mine... *Am I dreaming? Not this time, it's for real.* We fall on the bed; she lays down on her back. I run my hands all over her body and I start to kiss her body from her neck and slowly moved down to her beautiful breasts, kissing them, she is moaning. I then start kissing her belly and go lower, right to her fanny, all clean and shaved, and I start licking it. She opens her legs wider as she is loving it and it has a lovely smell. I can't stop, I am like a crazy man, pushing my nose in, licking and then some fingers. She is moving her arse up and down and still moaning softly. I moved down to her legs and kiss her feet, she then bent up, grabbed my head and pushed it at her fanny, she likes this so I carry on kissing it and rubbing it with my fingers. I need to come up for some air. She wriggles round the bed, put my hard cock into her mouth and was giving me a mind-blowing blowjob. It was good, I was moaning, holding her head as pushing all the way to take my cock in her mouth, she did. I then pulled her head away, pushed her down and laid on top of her. She then guided my cock into her fanny, I pushed back and forwards, slowly, and then we were moving together and I was holding her breasts. Then, this feeling came over me and I was ready to explode. She gave me an almighty push and said she was coming. We both came at the same time, it seemed to go on and on, both of us moving, with my cock still inside her. We just lay there, saying nothing, it felt as if I had known her all my life. We got under the covers and hugged each other. I just wanted to run my hands all over her silky skin. We then both got a bit touchy and we were all over each other again. Straight into sex this time, no messing around. She, on top of me, riding me hard and moving up and down. God, it felt good! We were at it for some time. I switched places with her and then, she whispered in my ear, "I want you to come in my mouth." So, she took a hold of my cock—still wet from being inside her—put it in her mouth, licked it, took it right down to her throat, grabbed it, winked at me and was wanking me. She then licked the tip of my penis, waiting for me to explode, one more lick and that did it for me. I shot my load straight into her mouth, she then sucked my cock till it was dry from cum and swallowed it all. This is every man's dream girl.

We just laid there wrapped into each other and fell asleep.

I had forgotten to set my alarm for an early call in the morning. I woke up and looked to see her but felt shocked, she was not there, she left a note on the pillow, it read: *It was a wonderful night with you. Had to go. We must do it again.* That's it, no phone number. Christ! It's seven thirty and I have a meeting. I need a shower. Washing my body and feeling good, so good that I felt like having a wank in the shower. But no, I will save myself. I finish the shower and suit up. Now I feel good. I dip down for some nice strong coffee and toast. That bloody waiter is smiling at me more now.

"Coffee, sir?"

"Thank you." I say.

He says, "Busy day today?"

"Yes, a meeting,"

He says, "Yes, I know too."

What is going on? Everyone knows what I am doing before me and where I am staying. I have this feeling in my stomach. I ask what is the date today. "The thirteenth of November," he says. This bloody thirteen is doing my head in. My mobile rings. It is Sonia. *Oh my God! What do I say to her? Keep cool.*

"Hello, honey. How are you?" she says.

"Hi. I'm at meetings all day, going to the factory and hoping to get some orders. But it is not going very fast with these people. They don't believe in it."

"Okay. Take care. Love you. Bye."

I am feeling shit right now and guilty. So, I take a deep breath and get up from my table to go up to my room. When

I am in my room, I come to remember about my camera and connect it to my phone to watch the playback to see if someone came in. Yes, it shows the maid cleaning the room, making the bed, then picking up my aftershave to have a spray, then sniff it. *Cheeky girl*, I thought, *so they do things like that*. Then she left the room and it showed blank for a while. But then I saw it. A man in a dark suit came in and started to look in my case and into the drawers that I had put some clothes into. This guy had gloves on and he started to look behind the pictures on the wall, then he went into the bathroom. He came out and left the room.

What is he looking for? So, I set the pen up again to record any movement in my room, then I left. As I came down the stairs, I saw the reception desk and saw a lady behind it. She looked up, smiled and said, "Good morning, Mr Johnson." I smile back, nod my head and sit in the lobby area waiting. It was about 8:45 a.m. So, I had time to think about last night and my time with Maria – good job. *I am fit and work out to keep fit.* Just then, a lady appears and calls my name. This was not the same girl as yesterday. I thought maybe it's her day off. So, I follow her. She opens the door and in I get. I open my laptop to check the details of what was talked about in yesterday's meeting. Well, today could be worth a lot of money. I am thinking of getting some orders, then catching a plane home. We are in lots of traffic again. I look up and see her looking in her mirror at me. I just smile, she does not say a word. Now we have been travelling for some time and then come to a factory. But it looked a bit run down. We stopped and I tried to open my door, but it was locked until the driver came to open it. As I got out of the car, two big suited men came to me. One said, "Follow us." (It seems to me that all head of companies have body guards. Well, this is Russia. So, I do.

We enter these big doors and turn left. I look around and see broken windows and a huge empty warehouse. This can't be it. What's going on? I am thinking there is nothing in this place. Is this a joke or what? I say to these two guys, "I think I am at the wrong factory."

"Follow us," came the reply.

We then go up some stairs and there are office doors. It all looks clean and tidy here. We walk a bit more, then they point to a door. "Go in," one said. I open the door, go in and see a big desk and chairs round the room. I sit on one. The two guys are standing outside talking. I could hear the conversation but it's in Russian. Then another door opposite the desk opens and two men come out. Behind them is a large, built man who smiles at me and says, "Good morning, Mr Johnson." I stand up and explain that I had a meeting with the CEO of the Heysel Group. "Yes, I know, and you were to be picked up at 9:00 a.m., but my car went for you. So, I guess your meeting will have to wait with the Heysel Group. My name is Cristian. That's all you need to know."

"Why am I here?" I shout.

"Calm down and I will explain. You own a company that deals in high tech electronics."

"Yes, so what?" I say loudly.

"Calm down, Mr Johnson, and I will explain. Oh, by the way, did you enjoy your last night with Maria?"

Now I'm thinking what is going on? He then says, "I don't think your girlfriend Sonia would be impressed. Do you?"

So that's why the man was in my room the first time, making it look like they were looking for something when my case was tipped out all over the bed. That was when they put a camera in my room, the second time was to recover it. These bastards! How on bloody earth do they know all about me and what I am doing? Now I am getting a bit agitated and I shout at this man, "What the hell is going on and what do you want?"

"Sit down and I will explain. You have been on our radar for the last two years. Don't worry about your 9:00 a.m. appointment. We have rescheduled it for two days later from today. Okay? And we have apologised and said you have a tummy bug." Who needs a PA when these guys are about? What I am thinking is that this man in front of me speaks with an American accent and I am getting confused.

Then this man with the name of Cristian, speaks clearly and softly, "Now, you are here in this country to sell your electronics, correct? And you will get the orders."

How does he know all this? I thought.

"Now, these parts your company makes are to go into missiles. They are a direction correction, is this right?"

"Yes," I say.

"So, well as you know, we are very concerned about this country building missiles as this could mean a threat to my country, which is America. I will explain about myself. I am with the CIA and we are concerned as I said."

"We want you to make these parts but not with a proper 'direction correction', or as we know it as DC, so they explode mid-air. Do you understand what I say? We don't trust that any of these missiles won't be pointing at us, so 'you' can help us. You will be paid a large amount of cash for your services. 'Do you understand?' Will you help us?"

"I will have to think this over. I am con...fused."

Then he says, "You have two days and you will not leave this building until we have signed a contract. And don't forget, 'we know all about you', like where you get your suits made right down to the aftershave you use. Now, shall we have something to eat?" he says. "Follow me, and I warn you, 'do not try to leave this building until I say so.' We are in the middle of nowhere and I have men all over this building, and I have a special area for you to see and advise me on." We go into another room and a buffet is laid out with food I recognise. He must have been shopping at Sainsbury, the coffee was good and I plated up some food. I don't know if I can eat at the minute as my head is banging and my stomach is rumbling. I force some down me and drink plenty of coffee. "You can sit a while and watch television," he says, "All English channels." He switches it on and there's the news. I am really not watching it. He then says, "I must go for a while. You rest and I will be back later and show you an area I need your advice on." Then he leaves the room and two suits walk in and stand at the doorway. I am fit but I don't think that I would mess with them. It seems that all these suits are all from America but could speak good Russian.

So now I have these people, asking me to sabotage my own products, and then sell them to the Russians. I have drunk enough coffee and sat and watched television and it shows that the euro lotto is at 113 million. *God! That number again,* I thought! I wish that I was not here. I don't feel good at all. I start to look round this room and notice a camera in the corner of the ceiling. So, I am being watched again. I thought of Big Brother. I look at my watch. It is 1:30 p.m. and just then my mobile rings. I take it out of my pocket to answer it when one of the suits jumps in and snatches it from my hand.

"What the hell!" I say, "Give it back."

He says, "Not allowed to have a phone. You will get it back when the boss says so."

"This is crazy. What next?" I say, then just on, he must have been looking at the camera and seen it and the main man comes into the room.

He speaks to the suits and they move to the other door. Then he says, "Follow me, please," and we follow the suits out through the door, turn right, along the corridor we walk and I see a lift that the suits open. The doors were metal ones that had to be pulled to one side. I stand there, then we all go into the lift, and the boss presses the floor button. It moves. We move up two floors, it stops. Then they all turn around, push the back panel, it opens up and we all walk out some secret door. They shut the panel and believe me, there is no evidence of a lift at all. We walk along a passageway, see a door and walk in. It is an area of about 12 by 12 feet with white overalls hanging up. I am told to put a suit on and head cover, plus the boots. We are all in white suits and I am just standing there. Cristian pushes a button on the wall and hey presto, a door swings open.

Then we go into a tall glass like tub in a round circle. It automatically shuts the glass door. I feel fresh air blown in and then an extractor taking the air out. Cristian says, "It is to take all dust particles away from our bodies." Nothing to worry about up to this point. No one had said a word. Then *whoosh*, the door opens and he says, "Carry on please." We step into a time warp – something out of Dr Who's Adventure. All I saw was bodies in white suits leaning over work benches. God knows who pays the electric bill if they do, as this place was lit up brighter than the Black Pool tower. Cristian beckons me to follow him. His two men, who are now in white suits, stay behind and just look at us moving. He introduces me to a small man in a white suit and Cristian says, "This is Professor Stein who runs this operation."

Professor says, "Follow me this way, please." He then goes through an automatic glass door, then into a further room as I look around. There are only four bodies working here. I thought to myself, this looks serious. Then we stopped and I heard Stein call out over the speakers, "Please answer the phone," and then just as I am looking at him, he pulls his sleeve up on his right arm and looks at his watch, if it was a watch. He stood still for a while. I got it! It is recognising his eye – the pupil. Then he speaks and voices talk back to him. Now I was not very far from him but tried to give him some privacy.

Then, while looking at him speak, I could see numbers tattooed on his arm, not going up but round his arm. Then I could see him moving this watch up a bit on his wrist. I thought no more of it. He then stopped talking and faced us and said, "I would like you to see this." We move about ten feet towards a bench with no one around it. He then picks up some electronic card and says to me, "Is this what you make, Mr Johnson?" I take it from him and look at this board, apart from our company's logo, it was exactly a copy of what we make. I nearly fell backwards thinking I had cornered the market that I had to hold onto the bench. I did not want them to think that I was shocked.

So, I smile and say, "Very good, but it has some parts missing."

Stein says, "Yes we know that you don't finish these. You do that just before it goes into the rocket or missile." GOD! They know everything! I, including the only two people at my company know about this. Also, we make other electronic pieces as well as dishes. It seems they have done their homework but left out what they don't know about the other items that I manufacture.

I must have a mole in my firm, that's where from they get the information. But Stein says, "We don't know about the final pieces, that is what you are going to show us. I understand you are with us for two days but that will be enough time!"

"Why should I show you that will finish my company?"

Cristian who has been watching and saying nothing, now opens his mouth and states, "You will build the parts so we can copy them and then, these will go with your orders when you send them to Russia and you can pick these DC up from us ready-made and fit them when required to."

"What if I do nothing and don't get the orders?"

"You will get the orders, no problem."

"You seem to be sure about it."

"Don't worry, Mr Johnson. All will fall into place. Now I must leave as you only have two days to make them," and leaves with his band of men.

The professor shows me to a bench with all kinds of special pieces that look just like the ones we use to make this component. I know from making these before, It's a long job.

"Now if you get started, we can finish and have some food. It's now 6:00 p.m.," he then says, "If you need any help, call for my assistant, Miss Putin. She will help you all she can. In fact, I will call her now so she can watch you working on the first card."

So over she comes, another white suit. Can't really see her face much as she has her hood up.

"Okay," I say.

"Hello." She just nods.

Okay one of these people who can't talk. So, Stein tells me to start and says, "Anything you need? Helga will get it for you." So now I have a first name. Helga Putin – no it could not be the president's wife, or daughter, I am dreaming again. Before he goes, he says, "I know that they have two missiles capable of reaching the USA. One is XVTl and the other is the XVT2. I will assume they will give you more orders to throw you off the scent as to what they really want them for." This is getting worse than I thought, it's for real. You only read a book or see a film with this crazy stuff. I put on my special glasses. These help to magnify things and I start to assemble my cards. It's a good job. I invented this and have done it from scratch before but it's a long job, very technical and small parts to solder together. Now as I start, I have to make two of these and then they will make more. Finally, they'll put them into some device to abort the rocket mid-flight.

I have been working for about an hour. Miss Putin looks over my shoulder, writes notes and says nothing. She was close to me but I could not smell any perfume. *Maybe not allowed*, I thought. Then the professor comes back and says, "Good. You have made a start. Have you written it down, Miss Putin?" She just nods her head. "Okay, we will go and shower and then have dinner. It's about 6:30 p.m." We go out the same way we came in—the glass tube—all three of us. We take our white overalls off and put them in a bin. Miss Putin is not shy and when she took off her overalls, she only had her bra and panties on, she had her back to me then speaks as if she can see me looking at her,

"It gets too hot in there all day," then puts on a jumper, skirt and shoes. She looked very pretty and slim. I put my suit back on but no tie. We open the door to the lift and go down two floors. Out of the lift, the other side and back into the corridor. Stein mentions that a shower is in my room where I will sleep. I mutter that I have no clothes to change into. Then Cristian appears and says, "Don't worry about that. We brought you some clothes from your hotel."

Is nothing safe here? I think. "Okay, thank you," I said.

"Miss Putin will show you to your room, dinner is at 7:30 okay?" said Cristen.

I follow her along the corridor then she says, "This is your room. If you need anything, I am right next door." What does she mean? The door is unlocked and I walk in. It's just like a hotel room, big bed, lovely furniture and a mini bar. I then look in the bathroom, very big bath and shower—separate and big.

By now I thought if there are cameras in here? But too tired to look and stripped off. I climb into the shower and freshen up; put on some casual clothes they had been kind enough to steal from my room. I look at my watch and it was 7:20 p.m. *Where do I go?* Just then there is a knock at the door. I go to open it and standing there was Helga, looking fabulous now. I could smell her perfume. She says, "Come with me to the dining room." Off we go, more corridors, then we go through double doors and into a room where there is a table laid out for six people.

"Would you like a drink?" she asks.

"Scotch and tonic please."

She nods to a waiter and says, "The same for me please. Let me try this drink as well." Then four people arrive. Stein, Cristian and his two suits. Stein must be high up on this list of people to have two body guards. I wonder if they sleep in the same room as him. That's why the six places.

"Please sit down everyone," Cristian says, "You sit near me, Mr Johnson." I don't mind as Helga sits opposite. At least something nice to look at while we have dinner.

Cristian speaks to me softly and says, "I just got off the phone with the President of the USA. He sends his regards and thanks you for your help."

Wow, I think. "Thank you."

"Don't thank me. You complete this and you are free." Then he says, "Look we cannot keep calling you by your last name. You know all of ours. What is yours?" speaking loudly so all can hear him.

I say, "My name is Rubin."

"Great, now we all know, and it is easier to talk now." I look at Helga who is sipping her soup. She looks back and smiles. We are served lots of food with an enormous dessert. It looked like jelly in a huge bowl with lots of cream and decorations on it. Cristian says, "You will like this as it is our special dessert. You must try some."

So, I say, "Yes, that would be nice." The waiter has his back to me when he dishes it up. I tried it and he was right, it tasted good; everyone had some.

"Now, Rubin, would you like a cigar and brandy?"

I say, "I will just have the brandy please, I don't smoke."

"Very good," he says and brandies are brought in for four people. The suits don't get any, they have to be on their toes I suppose. I sip my brandy and Stein who has been talking to the suits turns and speaks to me, "Now Rubin, how are the cards coming along?"

"Yes, fine. Thank you."

"Good, will we have them done in two days?"

"I would think so."

This is all very cosy but I hate to think if I had not cooperated. It's now 9:30 p.m., so Cristian says, "Well I think let's have an early night as we have a long day tomorrow." We all stand up and go through the doors. Cristian and Stein, with two suits, go another way to ours. I follow Helga from behind. *Nice view*, I thought.

"Okay Rubin, here is your room. Don't forget, anything you need, just knock on my door." I go into my room and fall on the bed. I am feeling drowsy. I should not feel like this after one brandy I thought! I must have dozed off on my bed when I heard a knock at my door. Before I could open it, it opens and I see Helga standing there. *No locks on these bloody doors!* She stands there in a see-through garment showing her bra, panties and stockings, it set my pulses going. *Am I lucky or what?* She says, "Can I come in?"

"Sure, what can I do for you?"

"Plenty," she says and enters the room and lays on the bed. Now she is not in the class of Maria but she looks good and I lay on the bed with her. She says, "How do you feel?"

I say, "A bit drowsy."

"Yes, well, you had sleeping drugs in your dessert," she says. That's why the waiter had his back to me and not the others. He put some into my dessert.

"Bastards," I say, "why was I doped?"

"It was to make you sleepy and keep calm, they don't like trouble makers here. They are dealt with. Not to worry, I had nothing to do with it. I swear Rubin. You are awake now, shall we start?"

I think, *Is this the American way?* So, I go into my bathroom and run the cold tap in the sink and wash my face to wake me up. I come back into the bedroom and Helga says, "Get over here and lay with me." I think, *What the hell? A man would not turn this down.* So, I lay on the bed and start to caress her. My hands go all over her body, she is smiling and says, "Carry on, I like it." Now do I wait for her to strip or have sex right away? I thought sex it is. So, I lay on her lovely breasts and great body then I feel a bump under my crotch so I put my hand down there and shock horror, *this girl has a dick!* I jump off and was just about to say something when she, or he, stopped me and said, "What is the matter, have you never slept with someone like me?"

"No, I have not and I don't wish to."

"Well can't we have a play about? I will please you."

"No means no. It's not for me!"

"Let me explain," Helga said, "yes, I am a woman in a man's body. I cannot afford the surgery, so if I do what I am asked to do, these people will pay for my surgery."

I now sit down. I said, "I see, but you could have warned me."

"What, and stop the fun? You did fancy me at first, didn't you?"

"Okay. I suppose you have the body and the looks, but not my scene."

"Well at least you did not scream. I have to stay here for two months or more and it gets boring, so it's nice to see a lovely fit man on bed with me." I go to the bathroom, turn the cold tap on in the sink and wash my face again. Trying to wash this out of my head and wake me up. Is she in on all this secret service thing? Did she get that sleeping powder put in my dessert so it might have been easier for me to carry on with her in bed? This is what I am thinking, but thank God I have never been in that situation. I come out of the bathroom and she is sitting on the bed so I say, "I need a drink. Do you want one?"

"Yes, please!" she replies very slowly.

"You can cut that out…" I said.

"I don't know what you mean, Rubin. What do you want to drink?"

"…or not. Yes please a vodka and tonic."

"Okay."

I do the drinks and share the tonic in my scotch. I then sit down and ask her what is going on and who are all these people.

"Okay, what I said about myself is true, regarding the operation for me, then you might want me Rubin—when I have had the snip," and she gestures with her hand like a pair of scissors.

"Okay, carry on, what about Cristian and Stein?"

"Well, Stein is here similar to me, he has his wife in jail in this country and they have told him that if he completes on time, they will get his wife free."

"Why is she in prison?" I ask.

"Well, she was a member of some freedom group, which was trying to get some of her family released from prison. Her father and uncle were over here and they got picked up. It seems for some silly charge, and it took ages for her to find out where they were. When she did, she came over here and tried to go public about their release. So, she also ended up in jail. Stein, who was still in America, working on a project similar to this, went to the embassy in his country for help. Then, the secret service got involved and explained to him where she was being held in Russia. They told him that if he came here for two months or more, they would get her and maybe the rest of the family released.

"I don't know much about Cristian. He is a law to himself and is high up and speaks to the President all the time."

"God," I said, "this is like a storybook tale."

"Now," Helga says, "you won't say anything to anyone about what I have told you. Right?"

"You have the voice like a female. I would never have known," I say to her.

"It was fun, wasn't it?" she says.

"No, it was not!" I say with a strong voice, "Anyhow, I think it's time you left. Don't you?"

"Okay Rubin, it's our little secret."

Yes, I think, *with loads of others to come.*

I have two days left to finish what they want done. She leaves and gives me a wink as she goes out of the door. *Good God! What am I into? This is a nightmare.* I take my clothes off, I put a chair and wedge it under my door handle, then I get into bed because I need a good sleep.

I sleep well at last. I get up, make some coffee, then shower and change into casual clothes. As I am wondering what this day will bring, I hear a knock at my door and Helga's voice saying, "It's time for the breakfast, Rubin. Are you ready?"

"Yes, now coming out." I go out to meet her.

"Good morning, Rubin. Slept well?" she says.

"Yes, good, thanks."

"Let's go, follow me." And off we go into the room we had dinner in last night. Although six placers are laid on the table, I only see Stein sitting down and he stands up when we come in.

"Help yourself to the buffet, and if you wish for hot food, then ask the waiter," Stein said.

I see the waiter and I put my hand up to beckon him.

"Yes sir, what can I get you?"

"Some scrambled eggs and toast, and coffee, please."

"Yes sir, right away."

So, I see Stein is eating a muse lay and Helga gets some salmon and ham and asks the waiter for tea. I notice Stein is not talking much so I start to talk to him,

"Have you worked here long?"

"No, not long," was his reply.

Then Helga speaks to say, "We have a busy day ahead. Don't we Stein?"

He nods and says, "Yes, I think so."

Then he stands up and leaves the room. My food comes. *They wouldn't have drugged me a second time, would they?* It all tasted good and washed down with coffee. Helga finishes and says, "We have to be at the lift at 8:45 a.m."

"Okay, see you there."

So, we walk back to our rooms and I just sit there. I don't know if thinking is good for the mind or not. It just makes your head go all over the place. I say to myself, *calm down Rubin and get a clear head.*

So, we meet up at the lift, just the three of us and off we go up two floors. Then, through the back of the lift and across to the changing room. Helga strips off facing me this time to bra and pants. When I look at her, I can't see a bulge in her panties. She must've tucked it into a sock. I smile. I strip down to my pants, she looks and smiles at me. "Oh, Mr Jonson." I just carry on and put my new white suit on and boots, pull my hood up and off we go into the bubble then into the glass door. We are now in the workshop area and I go to where I left off with her taking notes. Stein comes up to me and says, "When you get the two thirds of it done, I will then give you some other electrics to put in. So, don't finish it till I give you this. okay?"

"Right, got that." He leaves us. "He must think I am a robot," I say to Helga. Now there are other bodies working in here and they must have got in earlier than us. I don't know what they are working on so I ask Helga.

She puts her finger to her mouth and whispers, "I will tell you tonight." I hope she doesn't try that again with me. She must have guessed what I was thinking and said, "Don't worry, you're safe now."

I was working then Stein comes back and says, "Take a break. How are you doing?"

"Yes, good, I will be ready for your part later."

"Okay," he says, "Follow me," and we go through some doors to like a canteen area with food laid out. Nothing special, sandwiches and buns with hot drinks. We have about 30 minutes to rest, other people in white suits are sitting too, talking, but not in English. So, I did not understand but Helga could hear them and know what they were saying. But she says nothing to me. We had finished and stood up just then, Stein came in and said, "Follow me." *What now*, I thought. We go through some more doors, then into a glass tube to be hoovered again so, there is another door to come in here. Then, they open up and through some doors and we are back in the work shop. I thought that when we were walking back to the workshop, I could swear I heard a scream, I turned but Stein told us to carry on, so we did. I am working on my card system and get to the part; I have to stop and look up and move my specs and I see Stein looking at me. I tell him that I am ready for your part, so he tells me where he wants it but it has to be disguised in the card system somehow. He states, goodness know how I am going to do this, so I have to go on to their computer to look at the plans and work it out. This took me about an hour.

Right in my head I have a plan. I say to Helga, "I hope this works."

"It will Rubin, I trust you to do it." Well I'm glad she has faith in me, because I don't know yet if it all looks good on paper or the computer. Okay, here we go, I try one way, it does not fit, so I take it apart and you can see that this card has to be smooth, no jagged edges or anything high, it has to be level all round.

So, I try again, "What's the time?" I ask Helga.

She says, "5:00 p.m."

Right, let's do this, I look again and can see where I went wrong and start again. It's like a jigsaw, really all the pieces go in and all smooth, that's how I built these before.

So, I try again, going slower and thinking about each time I soldered a piece in. It looks good then some more in and bingo that's it, it's done!

I turn around and hug Helga she hugs back, smiles and says, "I told you so." As we turn around, guess what, Stein is standing there, a man of few words.

"All done?" he asks.

"Yes, I think we have it right. You can check it."

So, he picks it up by the edge, puts his glasses on and turns it over both sides and says, "Good, we will see if it works."

"What does he mean?" I whisper to Helga.

"You will find out at dinner."

He then says, "If you don't mind starting on your next one so we can get it done by tomorrow, as you have to leave, I understand."

"Okay," I say, "I will start and continue for an hour, after that, I will stop." So, Helga stays with me, the other white suits are still here working, so we do about an hour and I say, "I have had enough today, this is worse than working in my own place in the UK." She just smiles and gives a giggle. Off we go on our own into the bubble, then the changing room and out to the lift down. We go and walk to our rooms,

"See you soon Rubin,"

"Okay," I say and enter my room which has been cleaned and the bar stocked up with more than usual scotch. They must know it's my tipple, then I look around for a camera in the room, I did not find one but they could be anywhere. You need a sweeper to check the room for bugs and things and I did not have one as I did not think that I would need one. Oh, I don't care anymore, how worse can it get...

Right, I am showered and changed and just finished off with after shave. Then, I go out and bang on Helga's door, she says, "Come in." I just open the door and there she is, looking good, just playing with her hair. She asks, "How do I look?"

"Like a million dollars."

"Great," she says, comes out of the room and puts her arm through mine and off we go to the dining room.

We get through the doors and see Stein and Cristian talking but they stop when we enter the room. His two suits stand opposite to him. "Sit here Rubin, near me," Helga is sitting opposite me, smiling. Then the waiters come out with trays of mixed food. "You have a choice, Rubin. Some is Russian and some American." Rubin chases some off the American trays and watches what else does Cristian take? *If he eats it, I will eat it*, I think. So, we are eating away. I notice no wine, just water. Suits me, I have booze in my room.

Cristian turns his head to me and says, "I understand that you finished one of the DCs and added our components in it."

I say, "Yes. I think it will work."

He then stops eating, puts his knife and fork down and says loudly, "It better work. It's on its way to a missile as we speak, to be tested in the desert in Nevada. So, we will find out tomorrow if it's good or not. We carry on with the next one. Everything you do in the workshop has been recorded on film. So, we have you on record now."

"Okay," I say and think to myself; *I am not hungry*. He knows how to put you off your food.

"Tomorrow I would like a meeting with you before you start in the workshop. Helga will wait for you to take you in later."

"It does not give me long to finish the next one," I say.

"That's why you stayed behind, to start the new one." God, they have everything covered.

We have all eaten. During dessert, Cristian says, "Brandy, Rubin?"

"Yes, please," I say. So, four brandies are brought in and the suits stand outside the door.

"My men will come and fetch you at 8:30. Okay, Rubin?"

"Yes, alright," I nod. *No peace here*.

I can't go for a walk so we all stand up and Helga comes near me and says, "Shall we go? Do you want to come to my room or shall I come to yours?"

"I will come to yours but I will get some booze from my bar."

"Fine, I will be waiting," she says.

"None of that. You!"

I am laden with booze and knock on her door. "Come in."

I drop the booze onto her bed then she picks up some bottles and starts to pour the drinks, "Whiskey and tonic for you Rubin, and vodka and tonic for me."

"See, we have got something in common."

"Oh, what's that then? Tonic? You silly boy."

I told her that I feel safer in here. "Now tell me, what's going on in that workshop with the other white suits? And, where are they? I heard a scream earlier."

"Calm down, I will explain."

"Okay, I promise not to stop you, carry on."

"I had better top your drink up first," Helga says "Okay the white suits as you call them are all scientists from Turkey. They were caught in the USA, smuggling Mexicans across the border as they could not get work because they had no visa and were illegals themselves. They were put in jail, but were flagged up by the secret service. It pulled them out of the jail and offered the chance to work here in return. When the project finishes, they will be allowed to live and have a visa in the USA. They accepted the deal as they have families in USA. Now, the scream you heard, was on floor three as I understand. They have got some kind of area where they punish people who don't cooperate with the system. That's where Cristian is most of the time as these people who are in there are high flyers and this place needs them to work. If they don't then they get punished."

"Bloody hell! Never thought about that."

"Well," Helga said, "maybe it is a good thing you played ball with the system or otherwise you could have been in there."

"Cristian says I have one day left. I hope to get this done and leave."

"Oh, I will miss you, Rubin," Helga pouts her lips. I have had a few drinks and she still looks good. Her face, breasts and her body, they all look good. I think, then I say, "You had a lot of surgeries then, what about shaving?"

"No," she said, "I had injections for that and some tablets, which I still take every day, so my face looks good. I worked in the research in the USA for NASA. Once, I went into a bar all dressed up and started to chat with this guy who seemed very interested in me. We chatted and upon leaving he left me his card and told me to call if I needed a new job.

"Well, after a couple of months, I did ring him. We met up and he said 'I know all about you trying to change your

35

body and to do the rest, your surgery is very expensive and you have no money in your bank'. So, he tells me about this job in Russia for two months or more and that they will foot the bill for me to have the surgery if I come over here to work. Plus, I get some cash to start a new life when I get back to the USA and I have it in writing, a contract. So, now Rubin, you know everything about me. When I have had it done, will you look me up when you come over to the USA?"

"Maybe," I say.

"Okay, thanks for being straight with me, I appreciate it. Now I am off to bed."

"You can sleep here with me if you want."

I decline and get back in my room. I can't help thinking what is really going on here. Meeting with Cristian first, right after some coffee, then a shower and breakfast, there is a knock on my door. I shout this time, "Coming Helga." I come out and there she is, my wonder woman. We walk to the breakfast room. When we go in, I notice the table is only set for two. We sit, the waiter comes in and asks what we would like. I say, "Porridge please, and toast and coffee."

Helga is at the buffet getting salmon and ham she shouts, "Tea for me please!"

We sit down and eat and drink coffee. We have a small talk, nothing so that anyone can hear what we say. When the doors open, two suits come in and say. "Would you please come with us, Mr Johnson? Cristian would like to see you now." So up I get and follow them to his office.

I am outside his door and one of the suits says, "Go in." This was the office I first came in when we came into the building. I wonder if I could make the stairs and run outside. It's not far but there would be body guards about.

It's now 8:25 a.m. and I have to wait for 8:30 a.m. dead on time I thought. The other door opens and in comes Cristian with two suits, I am thinking he takes this job seriously no wonder he knows people in high places. He sits down and first thing he says, "It's a good day today, Rubin, isn't it?"

I say, "Yes."

He comments, "Well I told you a missile with your panel in it was fired over Nevada desert and with our amendments to the panel we were able to use your DC card and send it where we wanted so, success, Rubin, you should be pleased."

"So, let me get this right. You want me to alter all my panels that I get orders for, then, if a missile comes towards the USA, you will be able to send it into the ocean."

"I guess."

"So, it does not land on your soil."

"That's correct Rubin. So, you might be here a bit longer to make the DC to cover a longer range. Would that be possible?"

"Yes," I say, "All depends on the range you're looking at. Anyhow, I thought you had jets and others things to shoot these down. No, the president agrees with me and my team and he wants it done this way. We can make a large dish that can move in a circle and if it picks up any incoming missiles, we can direct them when they are in our airspace."

"Christ, I did not see that coming. How long do I have to stay now?"

"As long as it takes to build it and test it in the USA." I feel a bit pissed off now. "Okay, today you will finish that board you started. Then, you will work on a Direction Finder Plus for us. You might like to know that the President is very pleased that you are on board."

"Do I have any choice? You are holding me here against my will. Anyhow, I am supposed to be having a meeting with the CEO of the Heysel Group tomorrow."

"Don't worry about that Rubin. That's all taken care of. We have your plans, not all of them, and one of my staff will go to your place and apologise for your absence and say your tummy bug got worse and you are in a hospital in Moscow for treatment and if they check, your name is on the hospital list for treatment as we speak. Don't worry you will get some orders for your company I assure you."

"Yes, I might. But this is sabotage."

"Yes, it may be. But you are helping to keep our country safe from Russia. Next problem could be China."

God what next? This is like being wrapped in cotton wool. They have everything covered. I ask, "Why me? There are lots of people out there who are cleverer than me."

"Rubin, you put yourself down. You have an honours degree in your field and if I am not wrong, you got expelled from your private school for making flying machines and dropping mini bombs in the rest area. Plus, you used to make things with your father in his workshop. He was a great scientist your father. We think you have all the qualifications we need. You started your company from scratch and now it's worth millions.

"You better watch out in case someone wants to buy your company. You can do more than we need. We have you on film and Helga is by your side. She can advise you from her research and make notes. So please, don't try to sabotage anything as you will not receive a large amount of cash if you do so. We have other ways to persuade you but you will find them to your displeasure and Helga will not be very pleased with her outcome either. But, let's not talk about that Rubin as I am sure you will cooperate with us. Won't you?"

I am still thinking.

He says, "Again Rubin."

"Yes!" I say rather slowly.

"Thank you, Rubin." Just then he presses a button under his desk and the suits appear.

They say, "Follow us."

So, I stand up and turn to go when Cristian says, "Good man, Rubin. See you at dinner." *Fuck dinner. I want to get out of this asylum*, thinking to myself. The suits walk me back to my room and I go in.

I am sitting on the bed and Helga says, "How did your meeting go?"

With a grunt I say, "Not good. I have to stay here and do another project which means drawing up plans on the computer, then make it for real."

She says, "Goody, goody. We will be together longer."

I look at her and say, "Don't push it, okay? Are you ready to go into the workshop?"

"Yes, come on."

So off we go through all the rituals to get in the place. I did not even bother looking at her when we undressed this time. My brain was all over the place. We arrive at our area, she has a note book ready, don't know why as she wrote it all down yesterday when she watched me.

I start working on the board that I was on yesterday. I have been working on it for about an hour when Stein appears. "Good morning, Rubin, Helga." I look up and move my glasses. He says, "Now, that you are building the Direction Finder Plus, after this one you will start working on the dish that Cristian spoke to you about. The new dishes will have this component." He shows me the piece to go in the dish. "I have not even drawn up plans yet for the dish. I don't know what dimension it is."

"I will send Mr Roseburg in with the rough plans as he drew up some for us. It took longer than we thought. Oh, and if you need more help tell, Mr Roseburg to stay and help you, Mr Roseburg will come and assist you Rubin, he is a clever man."

"Yes okay," I look at him with content and he just disappears, no more words. I whisper to Helga, "I don't like this at all. Who is this guy Roseburg? I should have been out of here today. Now I feel like a prisoner."

"Don't talk now, we can talk later. Okay?" I nod my head, and carry on.

Now, I am thinking how long will I be here? No phone to use, everything is going the wrong way for me. It goes to show that Stein is close to Cristian, they must talk a lot about these projects. He must be second in command on all this workshop. What's going on in the other parts of this building, and how can they get away with living and working in this country that they want to knock out their missiles without Russia knowing? *Crazy.*

Right now, I have to get this panel done today. Helga is looking at me and can see that I have been drifting away, she says, "Snap out of it Rubin, let's do some work." I just look at her and nod my head. I then started to work and the glass door opens. I look up and through my specs and I see a white suit come in. I take no notice as I think it was one of the Turks who work on the other side to me.

Then, this suit comes to me and says, "Rubin?" with a tube under his arm. I thought what now. "My name is Roseburg and I was sent to you with these plans, for the dish you will be making." He looks at me, even though his hood was up, I could see his face and it was bloody and had bruises. When he passed me the tube with the plans in, he passed it to me with his left hand as I noticed his right hand was bandaged. He was not talking properly to me he had a problem with some words. I look at him and say,

"Thanks."

"Is there anything I can do Rubin?" It seems he does not want to go back anywhere in a hurry. I felt sorry for him and thought that could be me, if I don't do what is asked of me. I thought of giving him some little task to see if he can do it. So, I explain to him what I want him to do, he nods his head and says, "Okay." All this time Helga is watching and says nothing and I bet she is not the only one watching us. I carried on with my project for a while, then I checked to see how Roseburg was doing. He was struggling so I said don't worry old chap just watch me. After about five minutes the glass door opens, Stein appears and shouts at Roseburg,

"Come with me please!"

Then they both leave the area. *So, they are watching us,* I carry on after watching them leave.

I ask Helga, "What is the time?"

"4:13 p.m." she says.

"No, not that thirteen again." I am getting towards the end of putting my components in this card when Stein comes in and hands me his extra piece to add to my card. I say, "We have not even had a break today," and carry on. It's now about 6:15 p.m., I finish my card and stand back and scratch my head. Stein is still in the room and he comes over.

"Is it finished Rubin?"

"Yes."

"Okay, I will test it, then send it on," as he inspects the card. "Looks good. We shall see though. Okay, you better finish and clean up and have dinner."

"Shall we?"

Helga and I go to the glass doors and do the ritual of getting out of this place, then down in the lift, we walk to our rooms not a word was said between us until we approached our doors then Helga says, "I will wait for you."

"Yes, I say," as I am just pissed off with it all now. I have got to find out what is really going on or even escape from this place. I go into my room, all tidy, bar filled up and I make myself a drink. Then shower and sit down. It's about 7:10 p.m. so I knock on Helga's door and ask, "Are you decent?"

I hear her say, "For you, no! But come in dear boy, I still have my drink topped up in my hand." she says. "Sit down you have started drinking early!"

"I am pissed off. I should not be here. There is more going on than we know about Helga."

"I know," she says, "But I don't get involved, I just hear things and say nothing."

"Well I am going on a race tonight and will have a look around. You coming?"

"You must not do that."

"And what about Roseburg? Did you see the state of him?"

"Yes, I did."

"Do you think it was him screaming the other night?"

She looks at me and says nothing, then says, "Okay are you ready for the dinner?"

We go into the dining room and I see places set for seven people. Stein is already sitting. Helga and I sit together and then Cristian walks in with Roseburg and his two suits. Cristian points to a chair and says to Roseburg, "Sit near me and the two suits in the other seats this cosy," Then the waiters appear just like magic, with big trays, and start to deliver the food on our plates. It looks like liver, then mashed potatoes and kidneys then small round balls. When I ask what they are, I am told cabbage balls. I look at this food with distaste, then

41

I see that Cristian is looking at me. "Unhappy meals can increase stress levels Rubin. Don't you think?"

"Yes, I suppose so," I say.

"So, we don't want that, do we?"

"Fuck off Cristian," I say, "this is not the food for me." I can see Helga looking at me and pulling a face,

"Oh, what would you like Rubin? You are not eating hotel food now. Maybe buffet-style options mean everybody can enjoy a relaxing meal. Is that what you would say for all of us Rubin?"

"No, I am not saying that at all," He then turns and speaks to Roseburg.

"I see you are not fit for work yet, is that right?"

"Yes, it seems that Cristian."

"After dinner would you come and see me Rubin, in my office?" *Fuck! That will slow me down for having a look around this place.* So, for the rest of dinner it was quiet until asked for brandies, everyone says yes, then the suits go outside to wait for the main man. We all drink our brandies and stand up. I wait and hold Helga's arm tight so she can't move then. While she looks at me, I whisper to her that I would come to her room after my meeting. She nods and we leave. I am following Cristian and his suits to his office.

"Come in," he says while the suits stand outside. Then two more come into the room from the other door and stand there. "Now Rubin I don't want to hear any more outbursts from you in front of my guests."

"They are not guests, you are holding them all, with a promise to help them later on when this all gets finished. That is, if it ever does."

"Very clever," he says, "You seem to have found out things already. These people who work for me have an extremely high pain threshold. Now, we have not found yours yet Rubin, but if you don't do what is asked of you, we might have to find how high yours is. Do you understand? 'Do you understand!!!'" he shouts.

"Okay, I get the message. What I would like to know is why you did not build all these things in the USA? It would have been quicker and easier."

"Rubin, what you don't understand is this project could not have been built in my country, as, if this leaked out, it would have started a cold war. Besides, we did start on a small project with robots, and the objectives could not be met so, it was scrapped. Also, we own this factory and the land round it. At night, we have electric fencing that rises up from the ground to stop any intruders. We don't get much now after we found two bodies near the fence, because during day time it goes back into the ground to stop any snooping, from drones coming over or any aircraft.

"Plus, Rubin, if you try to escape from here you will hit our brick wall. You won't see it but you will know when you find it, that is automatically controlled to be live when the heat of your body gets near the spot where the wall starts. Plus, also, if my men see you outside this floor, they will shoot you."

"Okay, if I am killed what about your dish? Who will do it then?" I said.

"Shoot you, I did not say kill you, I am sure you understand now Rubin."

"You're evil," I said.

"So maybe, I have answered your questions and more. Now, at this time I understand from Stein that, Mr Roseburg is not fit to help you tomorrow. But he will be fine to work the next day after, we have patched him up better."

"How did he get those bruises and cuts."

"Would you believe he ran into a post?"

"No."

"Okay, let's say he would not cooperate with us at first but no problem now. He will be available to help with your mission on the dish very soon. You have completed your card today and that is being tested as we speak so that's good. Let's hope it does the same as yesterday.

"I remember you were asking why we need to do the dish. Well, this dish can or will be for long range at the moment. If we are lucky, we would get 10-15 minutes warning on average for our jets to scramble up into the air if a missile is fired at us from China, Russia, or from anywhere. With this dish, we can home in on it when missiles have been launched and done 300 miles. If it is coming our way, with your know-how and our components, we think we will have it sorted. But it will need to be tested first before you can leave. I am sorry Rubin."

Well, I have taken all this in. Anything is possible today if you have the technology to evolve.

I am now walking back to my room. This time I walk on my own they must trust me. I get to Helga's door and knock. "Come in," I hear, I go in. There was a drink already waiting for me. *What a girl*, I think.

"Sit down Rubin, you look tired."

"I am, and the shit I have just heard has worried me."

"What is it you heard?"

"Oh, I will say in a minute, but my thoughts are how we can get around this building to find out what else is going on?"

"Well Rubin, I can go around this place as I don't get stopped, so maybe I will do some snooping for you."

"Great, we will draw up a plan. Now what do you know about Roseburg, who is he?"

"Look Rubin, I can see you're tired and as much as I love your company, I still think we should call it a night. So, let's get some sleep. You can stay here if you wish."

"No thanks, I will see you in the morning."

"Night!"

"Night."

I stand up and leave for my room. When I am outside my room, I see Roseburg standing there. He says, "Can I have a word Rubin?"

"Yes, come in my room."

Can I trust this guy? Has he been sent to me on purpose? Straight after I had a meeting with Cristian? I say, "Sit please, would you like a drink?"

"No thanks," he said. I noticed he was in a sling for his right arm and his face was still marked.

He kept on looking at the door as if he was waiting for someone to enter. This made me feel uncomfortable. "What can I do for you?" I ask.

He starts talking, "Do you know, since I knew Cristian, all I have heard are blatant lies and utter drivel. I know you are going to be working on the creation of new scientific technology that will transform the dish. Is that right Rubin?"

"I guess so but first explain how you got here and why?"

"I am from Albania, not a wealthy country, I was a scientist working in India." Before he had said anymore, I hear someone outside. "Yes, I think I better go." So, I open my door, and look around outside. No one is there.

"Come on," I say.

"I promise to tell you everything the next time we meet okay?" It's clear outside and off he goes to his room. I guess. I am thinking this over, this is more than what Cristian keeps telling me and it is making my head ache. I get into bed and fall straight to sleep.

I needed that sleep. Woke up around 7:15 a.m., no television in our rooms maybe so that we don't watch any news. I get some coffee and have a long shower. Then I change and sit down for a while. I hear some noise coming from Helga's room and it gets louder with shouting. I get up to go out of my room and there are four suits outside standing there. One tells me to go back inside my room. I shout, "Why are you in Helga's room?"

"Just go back inside your room."

I am pacing up and down. When it all goes quiet, there is a knock at my door. Before I can say 'come in', the door opens. There is Helga standing there, crying. She comes sobbing towards me and puts her arms around me. What do I do? Hug like a male friend would or a deep hug you give to a female that you're attracted to? I am in the middle and just hug, and ask, "What is going on?"

"They ransacked my room thinking that I had a mobile phone hidden."

"Where did that information come from?" I ask.

"Don't know, they said you gave it to me to hide, but they found nothing and now my room is a mess."

"Don't worry, I will help you tidy it later."

"They might do your room when you are working Rubin."

"Well I ain't got nothing to hide. Now dry them tears and we will go to breakfast." The only meal you can eat, it seems.

We go in to sit down for breakfast and there sitting already is Cristian and Stein, the two stooges, and Roseburg. This is unusually full, don't normally see these many for breakfast. Maybe been up early, had a meeting or waiting to see if they found a mobile phone. Who knows? The waiter had served them already so I guess they were waiting for us to come in. The waiter takes our orders and we are eating the food, then Cristian speaks, "Good morning to you three. I hope you slept okay. It has come to my attention that there is a mobile phone being used in this building without my permission. How do I know this is because my sounder office reports to me about anything that is not on my agenda? We will find it soon."

"I don't know what you mean Cristian."

"Rubin, don't piss me off. You know what it means. If anyone has used a mobile, we will be able to track it and find who you have called. Do you understand now Rubin?"

"Why look at me? It's not me. Your goons took mine away from me."

"Well I am saying don't let me find one near you because you will know the consequences," and looks straight at Roseburg, "Is that right?" He just nods his head then the four of them get up and leave.

I look at Helga and we both look at the sorry state of Roseburg, who is struggling to eat his food with his hands shaking. "Well we have a busy day, Helga. I don't think you are joining us today, are you Roseburg?"

He shakes his head and says, "No, not today, I'm afraid."

Now what I can make out is that they are worried if someone rings the outside world. I am concerned that I might not get out of here alive. There are other things going on here, it is such a large factory, and floor three seems to be the key to some answers. I must try to get on that floor to see for myself. I will explain to Helga what I am going to do, I think I can trust her. Roseburg was going to tell me more; I need to find where his room is before anything else happens to him. Right now, I will do what they want but slower working on this dish. As I see it, the suits are all over the building and there are cameras in places. There is more to this, we can't be on Russian soil without them knowing something, what is going on in this place?

Right now, Helga and I are off to the lift on our own so when we get into the lift instead of pushing for the fourth floor, I hit the button for the third, "What are you doing Rubin?"

"Just wait and see."

When we open the door, we are at floor three. I open the door and step out and I see big doors in front of me so I walk towards them and push them open. To my horror, I see a missile laying on a bench. I am gob smacked, then someone grabs my arms. It's the two suits grabbing me and pulling me back to the lift. They throw me in, and press floor four and shut the door to the lift. All this time, the suits don't speak a word. Didn't have to really, action speaks louder than words. "What did you see?"

"A huge missile being built. I will tell you later, there is more going on than we know."

"Okay we will talk later."

Then we come out of the lift, into our changing room through the bubble, through glass doors and we are in. Stein is standing there and comments, "A bit late today, are we?"

"We went the wrong way."

"Oh dear," he said. "Right! Shall we start then?"

God, I wish I was not here. It's easy to get in but harder to get out. I make a start; I have to work on a different bench to make my parts and I am not far from the white suits who are always in here it seems. We need to speak to them as they must live on a different floor than us. So, I am slowly cutting my parts out and checking my plans, Stein is still standing there, watching me, he says, "How long do you think it'll take to finish it Rubin?"

"I really don't know, as you want this made and assembled, then taken apart to reassemble it again wherever it's got to go to. It only has to be a millimetre out and it won't work so I can tell you now Stein, it is not a fast piece of work. So, if you need to report that to Cristian, go ahead." Helga looks at me and smiles, that was enough to say, 'good for you'. I smile back and then work on with the dish.

I think, *right I will fuck this up, I am going to cut a piece too small.* I still don't know why I am doing all this by hand when there are machines that will get it right quicker than me.

Tonight, I am going to floor number three to check on that missile. It was bloody large, probably long range, but what is it doing here?

I say to Stein, "Why can't we have some music playing?" I will find out if this is allowed, maybe not in case they are listening, I thought. Now I have been here a few days and my office has not heard from me still so maybe Lauren will call the Heysel Group and ask them, maybe. Do we leave this place in a box, or can we walk out free?

It is a good thing that I have Helga for company. She keeps nudging me on purpose in a playful way, and keeps me sane. We work all day, no breaks, not even the other white suits. It came to 4:00 p.m. when Stein comes in and says, "Enough for today, you two can go and clean up. I know it's early but we can see some results." *Yes*, I thought.

We take our time in changing, they probably throw these used overalls away or burn them. Helga goes in her room and just before she goes, she says, "Rubin I will come to your room as soon as I am ready."

"Okay."

Off I go and look at my room. It's nice and clean, all tidy. I lay on the bed, head on my pillow, as I turn my head a piece of paper falls to the floor. It's really small, I pick it up thinking the maid or whoever cleaned the room dropped it. I pick it up and see the message on it saying, *meet me at 10 p.m. outside the lift on floor three don't use the lift stairs will be safer.* Well it's not from Helga. Who else knows me? This is what I think about when I'm in the shower. While I am putting my clothes on, I hear a knock at the door and Helga comes in.

"Do you mind?" I say.

"Oh, I have seen it all before."

"Yes, but not mine."

"No, not yet Rubin."

"Shut up and sit down." She looks at him before she could speak again. He handed her the message.

"God! Rubin, what are we to do?"

"What do you mean we?"

"Yes, we are both in it, let's do it together." Now we know that there is a missile, well, it looks more like a rocket for long range. Now a message. "Okay, let us go to the dinner Rubin." Helga thought Cristian will want a word about going on to floor three. We approach the door when Roseburg is coming towards them.

"Hold the door, please," says Roseburg.

So, all three go in and Cristian says to Rubin, "Sit near me." So, we have a table of six including the suits and Stein. Well, what a change to the menu, all wholesome food is served up. Then, Cristian speaks to Rubin saying about how far he has got on with the dish and that he is pleased with the progress, "You see it's easy when we all work together."

He won't be pleased when it won't fit together, he thinks to himself. Then it came to brandies all round but before Cristian could drink his, a suit comes in and whispers in his ear. He apologises and leaves the room. I nod to Helga to drink up or leave it, then we leave and go back to my room.

I make us a drink and we start talking about our rendezvous later tonight.

"Maybe we will find out more about this place."

"Yes, I hope so."

"Look Helga, if you get caught it will mean no operation for you."

"That's okay, what you don't have you don't miss."

"What about you and the money they promised you?"

"It's only money, I think our lives are worth more. Don't you?"

49

"You're right."

We are talking away, then I notice the time,

"Okay, let's hope there are not any suits around. Let's go."

We shut the door softly and start towards the stairs looking around all quiet. We proceed up wide stairs so we take one at a time to the next level. Then, the next steps, up to the floor three. It looks clear so we go to the lift, no one to be seen. Are we being set up? I am thinking how long do we wait.

Then coming along the other way to the lift I can see Roseburg walking with a suit in tow. Oh no, has he been caught, was it him who left the message? "Get behind me Helga, so you cannot be seen." I don't like the look of this.

They come closer and Roseburg looks at me and says, "Thank you for coming." I am amazed. *What does he mean?* He is with one of the suits who I have seen before. Roseburg speaks, "This is Sonny, an American, and has a lot to tell you."

Sonny speaks, "Now what you have to know is that we have about 15 minutes, as that's when the eyes are back to watch their screens. Everybody who works here are defecting to Russia and all that goes on in here is for Russia, not the USA. The Kremlin, which is over the river knows all about this operation. That's why we don't get any visitors, only number 13."

"What?" I say. "13?" I knew that number would crop up some time.

"He is in charge from the Kremlin, he does not come here often. What you need to know is that these missiles and rockets are for Russia. One missile or rocket is going to be launched against China and one against America. They will not be sent from here. Now, you Rubin, saw that rocket through the doors. Good thing I got to you first so Cristian did not know. Don't worry about the other suit he does what I tell him. Now, I am a true American and I am working with the CIA."

Helga butts in and says, "So 'you' are a double agent we read about. How exciting."

"Yes, something like that," he says.

"Now we have not got much time, I will let you know our next meeting and see if we can all come up with a plan. I have informed the CIA of your names and you will get our protection, okay, we better go now."

Off we go sneaking back down stairs back to my room. I ask Helga while pouring a drink, "Do you think we can trust them or are we being set up?"

"I don't know what to think Rubin. What is it he wants from us?"

"I think we still need to do some looking around to check things as to what is in these other rooms. It all sounds wrong, and that bloody number thirteen, who is that?"

We look at each other and confirm it's bedtime so she leaves and I lay on the bed and wonder what I have gotten into, while not forgetting to wedge that chair under my door handle.

When I wake up, I make myself a coffee and have a shower. I change while thinking about my meeting with Sonny. I hear a knock on the door,

"It's me, Rubin, ready for the breakfast." I move the chair and go out into the corridor. We walk together into the breakfast room. We go in and see Roseburg sitting down, no one else so we just nod to him. He nods back.

"I must say you look a lot better today Roseburg."

"Yes, I am good and I shall be with you today working on your dish."

"Oh, good," I say, then thinking he will find out about my inaccurate sizes on the dish. Well I will find out now if I can trust him. We finish breakfast then leave, we go to the lift and press the button, all three of us in the lift up two floors then we all go through our ritual of suits. The blower then the doors. At that time no one says a word. We just look at each other. When we get to our work station, Stein is standing there and says, "Morning all! We have a busy day and it will be good if this dish can look like it will be finished soon."

"I will do my best," I say, and then Stein leaves us. I show Roseburg my drawings and then point to the piece that has been cut and which is too small, he measures it and doesn't say a thing even after knowing it is too small to be fitted. I think he must be on our side and we can trust him. I give him the thumbs up and he nods with a smile. Helga watches his reaction and smiles too.

We carry on working together and he is very good at what he knows and can promote it with his hands. We work on and get more pieces cut and it is coming together but, we still have the components to make the hardest part of this. *Now who is this dish for?* I think, Russia, not the USA. In case they get dragged into a cold war, they will be protected from the other country's attacks. As Cristian is now working for the enemy. Does he not feel any shame? These people now take a warped delight in bad news. Now I am dragged into this and there could be serious repercussions for my country. If it was found out that I have been helping the Russians to make a war between China and the USA, I would be locked up for life and I don't see how I can get out of this.

We are working on this dish and cracking on but it has not been put together yet. The next job will be to work, on the components but not today as my head is not thinking straight and we have to come up with some sort of plan to stop this madness. We really waste some time then Stein comes in, looks at what we have done and says, "Well done, we are getting there. When do you think it will be finished?"

"Maybe in a few days, it's hard to say, but we are close, then when it's done, we need to test it, don't we?"

"Don't worry about testing the dish, it will be moved to our testing site elsewhere."

"Where's that?" I ask.

"Don't you worry about that Rubin."

We three start to leave for the night, then Stein asks me, "Has Roseburg worked okay with this project Rubin?"

"What could I say? I don't know the guy really, so yes, he has been very helpful and he knows what to do as well."

"Very good, I will tell Cristian of your comments. You have fitted in well Rubin and you are trusted by us so don't do anything silly to spoil things. Okay?"

I smile and nod. *They trust me?* A man that cannot go anywhere and is spied on all the times and held here against his will. Helga grabs my arm and says, "Are you coming Rubin?"

"Yes, let's go."

As us three are getting out of our overalls, Roseburg whispers to me,

"9:45 p.m., in your bedroom, we will come for a meeting. Okay?" I nod and Helga looks at me and I put my finger to my lips she just nods. We go to our rooms and I think, *Fuck all this, it's cloak and dagger stuff and I have a feeling someone could get hurt here, I hope it's not me.*

Helga and I go for dinner and see five people in the room already, and it seems they are waiting for us. God! This looking at each other makes you feel uneasy. The waiter comes in, must have been waiting for us and we all order from him after he tells us what food is available. Well the menu is picking up; it must have been my outburst about the food to Cristian. After we finished the food, no mention of brandies, Cristian said his apologies and left with Stein and the two suits. A bit weird I thought and looked at the other two who just stared at me.

We get back to our room and Helga comes in, Roseburg went to his room. I still don't know where his room is. We had a chat about nothing really and waited till the other two came to my room. The time was 8:43 p.m. and there is a knock on my door, it was Roseburg and Sonny.

"Come in, sit down."

"Drink anyone?" Helga shouts.

"Yes please."

The other two decline. After an exchange of polite but cool pleasantries, Sonny starts to say, "Did you know, in Cristian's office, through the doors behind his desk is an office of veneer panelling? It all looks the same but on the far wall, a panel moves. There is a bomb-proof, steel-made bunker. There is a key pad entrance with biometric finger prints scanner. Only three people have the code and the finger print clearance and there are always two suits in the office to stop any attempts to enter that special room. If anyone attempts to break in, it will explode.

"Also, you need to know that Russia will take one missile and one rocket in a submarine and will stop in the South China Sea. Then, they'll launch the missile at China. At that time, the sub will launch the rockets towards America. Both have a variety of systems designed to cloak its presence in the air, including low-probability of radar, so both countries will think each other did it and Russia can keep out of it, looking safe.

"They will then have your dish Rubin, to track any missiles and divert them away, should any one fires any to Russia. Russia's alibi will be that they are working on a space programme as theirs is in a state, and they want a 30-day-stay in the mother ship which is in orbit."

"Makes you wonder where all the money comes from?" Helga says.

"It is oil! That was stolen from the companies and made national. Then sold off to the racketeers and now, the money appears all over the world. Buying properties and other investment in football clubs, you name it.

"I think that I have told you what I know. As Roseburg's room is near mine, I will pass any information to him to tell you. Just one thing, if you two go back on the third floor, that area you want to go in, with the rocket, that area overlooks Cristian's office. Now we must go the curfew with be on soon. Bye."

Both leave us.

"I think I need a drink now. You want one? A drink Helga, I mean."

They are both sitting on the bed in Rubin's room, when Rubin says, "Why are we doing all this here? It could be made anywhere. I am not happy about being locked up and made to do something that could start a war which is out of our hands."

Helga said, "Maybe not. If we can get to the rocket and check it over with Roseburg and you carry on with your dish to prolong things, what we don't know is there a date for all this to be finished."

"God Helga! Where does all your thinking come from?"

"I am brainy, that's all."

Rubin not just has looks but also a good body.

"I think it's time you left, Helga."

"I don't owe you, spoil sport Rubin. Bye." She stands at the door and says, "Don't leave me behind when you make your escape plan to get out of here. Please Rubin, promise me."

"Okay," I say, "I will not leave you behind, Helga. I promise."

She leaves the room; I can now try to hatch a plan to get us of this hell hole. Why is my company not contacting with them? No orders to process and it's costing me money and my valuable time being here.

I need to ask Cristian some questions to see if he can give me some information about this programme. It looks like there are more people working here than I know about. Have they all got a secret to hide from others and only Cristian knows their past history? Nothing here is as it appears.

I wake up in the morning and do my normal routine, coffee, then shower. I have put some fresh clothes on, at least it has a good laundry service here, never seen anyone come to my room to clean it. Do the cleaning staff stay on site or go home? They must come in when we have gone to work in our workshop.

We go to breakfast. Only three of us are there – Roseburg and we two. We decide to just exchange pleasantries and smile a lot. When we were leaving the breakfast room there were two suits still standing on the door. Maybe they were asked to report it back to the boss if they heard anything from us. I guess the room is bugged.

I turn to one of the suits and say to one of them, "I would like a meeting with Cristian, please."

"What about?" he asked.

"My business. Thank you, I will be waiting." And off we go to get ready for work. Roseburg and Helga look at me but say nothing. We meet at the lift and all three of us go in. *No suits around here* I am thinking. We go through the ritual of getting ready, then go in the workshop to make a start. We start on our dish and Roseburg is talking to me, but I don't hear a thing as I am thinking of what I shall say to Cristian. Just then, I get a nudge from Helga. She then said, "Roseburg is talking to you and pointing to the dish and where the components will be fixed."

"Okay," I say, "sorry, please tell me again."

We carry on with the suggestions and the time is ticking away. It's now just before our break time when we hear over the speakers,

"Would Rubin please come out of the workshop as he has to see Cristian?"

Great, I thought so off I go to get out of here. When I get out of the lift, a suit is waiting for me and just beckons me to follow him. He knocks on Cristian's door and wait,

"Come in!" I hear, the suit opens the door and wave me in, the suit stays outside. "Sit down Rubin, what can I do for you?" He sits behind his desk God knows what he has in that desk. Plus, another male is sitting at the edge of his desk. "Let me introduce Mr Wingers from MIS." I am in shock, now we have top brass from the UK in this mess? What next?

"Okay Rubin, what did you want to see me for."

"Well I am wondering how long I will be here and the orders that I came for from the Heysel Group have I lost them? Plus, I have not seen daylight since I've been here and how many days have I been here." I am just saying what comes into my head.

"Okay Rubin, let me explain to you. First of all, you have secured a big order for your products, which will increase later on if they are happy with the first ones you send over to them."

"How have you done that?"

"Never mind, its done and waiting for you on your return to the UK. I will look into you and Helga going outside for some different scenery."

I say, "Okay."

"You have been here for seven days so far. You can go when you finish your dish."

"What about Helga and Roseburg and the other white suits in the workshop."

"They are not your concern Rubin; they have a different contract than yours."

"Yes, about contacts, I did not see mine. How much are you paying me."

"Well Rubin, if you complete your task and there is no problem after testing. When you leave we will put 1 million dollars into your bank account."

"I thought it would have been more than that."

"Don't push it Rubin. I need you to finish your dish so we can show it off at our parade next week, so you have six days."

No! not again! I am thinking 6 plus 7 is that dreaded 13 again. It shows up all the time, I have to get out of here now I can't wait.

"You may leave now Rubin if that's all."

"Yes, thank you."

All the time, Mr Wingers is looking at me. Now, I know how the Russians found out about me if I had MIS watching me and passing the information on to Cristian.

I walk back to my room and see the door is open. I walk in slowly and see a lady making my bed.

"Sorry sir, I thought you were not here until later."

"No problem. Do you do this every day?"

"Only five days, then someone else comes in to cover me."

"So, you live outside these premises then?"

"Yes sir. I live 20 kilometres away. The people here like it if you live close in case you are needed at any time."

"What time do you work from?"

"9:00 a.m. to 4:00 p.m.," she says.

"I guess that you clean lots of rooms in this place then and that you know your way around."

"Yes sir."

"Listen, do you think you could draw me a plan of this place? I will pay you and I promise not to tell the bosses. It's just that I need to find my friend. Look I have to go back to work, when it's done, leave it under the pillow and I will leave you some money tomorrow or do you want the money now?"

"Yes, please sir,"

So, I go to the wardrobe and search under some shoes and put my hand in one and find some dollars. I give her 100 dollars, she is well pleased and says, "Thank you I will do it for you."

I leave the room and go into the lift thinking she will do it or tell the boss about it. I could not see any suits about they must trust us now on our own. I get back into the workshop and smile at Helga and Roseburg I am the cat who's got the cream.

"What's with you?" Helga says.

"Tell you later," and I whisper to Roseburg, "Meet in my room with Sonny at 10:00 p.m. okay?"

He just nods and smiles. He knows I have a plan; well I hope I have.

The rest of the day passes quickly. Haven't seen Stein all day. When it comes to 5:00 p.m., we decide it's time to leave. Through our changing room and finally in the lift then out.

I say to them, "Can you hear that someone's screaming?"

They both confirm that they can. We go back to our rooms to clean up. I cannot wait to get into my room to see if the cleaning lady has left me a plan or not. "See you later," I shout to Helga. I go into my room and lift the pillows and no plans or message. "Bastard," I shout. She took my money and nothing else. *Has she reported me?* I am thinking.

I just nod my head and think how stupid I have been. I will be caught. I make myself a drink and sit down with it. One gulp, then I get in the shower. As I am getting ready, I wonder if she saw me get the money from my wardrobe and took all my money. So, I quickly pull my shoes out of the wardrobe and search inside them and pull out my money. It's safe, then I check one more shoe and feel something. I pull it out and see it is some paper, as I open it I see a plan of the building. Great! she did do it for me. I put it back in my shoe and go and knock for Helga, when she comes out I have a smile on my face, and just put my fingers to my lips and whisper to her, "Tell you later okay."

"Whatever," she said.

We go into dinner and see all the seats plus one more for Mr Wingers, who is sitting next to Cristian, he has his favourites next to him. He looks is in a good mood and he speaks to me and asks,

"Have you had a good day Rubin? I understand you did."

"Yes, thank you."

When I look around properly I see Stein at the end of the table I have to look twice at him as his face swollen with red marks on it. I also noticed when he lifted his arm he was struggling to lift it, was it him we heard screaming. Maybe it was for us to see him in this state to warn us off if we did not comply, it was not nice to look at and it was silent for a while not how a dining room would be normally.

So, I ask Mr Wingers, "Are you enjoying your stay in Russia?" He looks at Cristian, then me and speaks,

"Yes. Thank you. I have some business to do here then back to the UK."

"Yes, I am thinking what bloody business is that then?"

"Something to do with the rockets."

I don't say anymore until Cristian says, "Brandy everyone?" We all nod, and I can see from the corner of my eye that Stein is in pain. So, I turn my head towards him and ask him if he feels unwell. As he is looking back at me, Cristian butts in and states that, "Stein has stumbled down the stairs and that has what caused his injuries. Isn't that right, Stein?"

Stein says, "Yes, that's right."

"And that is why you have not seen him today."

I look at Helga with the look of 'let's get out of here'. We stand up and say our good byes. As we leave, I can see Stein, his eyes looking at me, he wants to talk I can feel it. I need to get to him somehow, maybe the plan will say what room he is in.

Helga follows me into my room, I just pour us some drinks and we both sit down and start to talk. The first thing she says is, "What about Stein? What is all that about?"

"We need to find him and ask."

I go and retrieve the piece of paper out of my shoe and show her.

"What are you going to do with this?" she asks.

"This is our way of getting out of here. Do you want to get out of this building and come with me? I am guessing Roseburg, and Stein, will come too."

"When are you thinking of."

"Well, in six days they have the victory parade for all the arm forces in Russia. Vladimir Putin watches it all with all of his main men who work for the Kremlin and that includes Cristian now, and also this man only known as number 13 who overseas this operation. So, my plan will be to get out on that day. What do you think?"

"My guess is that there will not be many suits about and hopefully Sonny will help us."

"I just don't want to go but I want to leave a present for them after we get out."

"You seemed confident Rubin, are you sure about this and who you can trust at this time?"

"I only trust you Helga."

"Thank you Rubin, I think we have a bond."

"Yes, as a brother and a sister, nothing else, you understand?"

"Yes."

"Okay, well we have the other two coming soon. Maybe we can get our heads together and get this plan together for real."

I did not realize the time when there is a knock at the door and Sonny and Roseburg come in.

"Drinks any one?" asks Helga.

"Yes please. Scotch on the rocks for me and vodka for Roseburg," Sonny says.

"How do you know his drink?"

"We are old friends. I will explain, about two years ago we worked together for the CIA on another project in Pakistan. To try and find a man called Nan who was running a bomb factory for the Taliban. Roseburg is a scientist, so he was recruited in his field and I was working in security for them. It took us seven months before we even saw that man. He was a nasty piece and did not take to outsiders much, but we kept our heads down and carried on. We knew he did not trust us so he was around to watch what we did every day for a month.

"To cut a long story short we saw him on his own and our orders were to kill him whenever possible. Well, I did, with a knife, so no sound and sat him in a chair to make him look like he was asleep. Then we had a rendezvous with a helicopter and left sharpish."

"Okay," says Rubin, "can we trust you two? As I have a plan to get out of this place." I explain and show them my map of the building. "I want us to leave on the parade day." They are listening and nodding. "What is your input to this?"

Sonny starts to talk, "Okay my orders are to blow this place up so it can't produce any more rockets or missiles to start any wars or kill any more of the population."

"When are you thinking of doing this?" Rubin said.

"I know there is the parade in six days. Would that not be a good day so we can all get out at the same time?"

"Yes," Sonny says.

Rubin starts to talk, "I have had enough of this place. So has Helga. I need to find Stein to see if he wants to leave. It looks like he has had a beating. Look at this map of the place," and he shows them his piece of paper with the rooms on and stairs. "I am going to sneak out tonight to see him, his room is on this piece of paper. I don't know what he will say. He could report me to Cristian."

Sonny starts, "This is what I think. I need to get Cristian's finger prints to disarm the rocket. I could get them off his glass when we have brandy. Then I need to get in the basement to find some explosives and place them around the building. Roseburg can help me." He looks at him. He nods,

"Okay we have six days."

Then Rubin says, "And how do we get out of here?"

"Don't worry, I will call for a chopper to pick us up and drop us somewhere safe."

"Anywhere safe in Russia?"

"No, we go in the dark and fly to Albania. That is my plan. Anyone with any other ideas?" No one says anything. "Best of luck with Stein, Rubin. Don't tell him anything of the plan."

"It is between us four, none of this is going to be easy."

"When do you think your dish will be finished," Sonny asks.

"We are trying to hang it out but Cristian is pushing us to get it done by the next week."

"We better get going, talk to you later. Bye," we whisper and off they go, Sonny and Roseburg.

We sit down and Helga says, "I guess I will have to wait for my operation now."

"Listen to me, if we all get out in one piece, I will pay for your operation myself, so don't worry."

"Would you really do that for me Rubin?"

"Yes, I will! I think it was Sonny who used that mobile and he must have used it near our rooms, so let's hope we can trust him, maybe we need to think of a plan in case there is a problem, what do you think Helga?"

"I think you're right to have a backup plan Rubin. You said we have six days, maybe we need to do some praying."

"Well, I am going out to find Stein."

"I want to come with you Rubin. I would not be able to live with myself if you got caught. We go together or you don't go, I mean it."

"Okay we go in 30 minutes."

We try to put dark clothes on. It was not bright in the corridors. They had put the night lights on, so here we go. I look at the map and tell Helga to keep to the sides, we are taking a big risk but I am curious and want to speak to Stein. We slide past several doors, trust him to be the furthest away. I check my map and see that he is two doors to go that's when we hear a noise from behind us. I point to Helga to hide and I do the same. We can just see it looks like the white suits are going back in their own rooms, we wait then mov on until we arrive at Steins door.

I tap on his door and nothing, I tap again, I try the handle and the door opens so we go in and shut the door. The light is on and there are papers on a desk, when I look at them I can see it is a plan for the rocket and missiles, he knows his stuff, as he has made notes on more paper. Helga looks around and says, "Where is he? Do you think he is in a meeting with Cristian?"

"We will have to hurry." I am writing all this information down; I would like to take all of these plans and notes but better not. Helga makes a noise and I look at her, "Don't make so much noise."

"Look at what I have found, a gun with extra bullets," she whispers. "Shall we take it?"

"Yes, we shall. Okay, let's move out of here." We open the door and look outside and see the suits doing the rounds. So, we wait, breathing deep and putting our hands over our mouths to keep quiet. Then we move out on to the corridor, just then, a shot rang out, then another one. We look at each other and move towards our rooms with baited breath, we head straight into my room, shut the door and I wedge a chair under the handle.

"Oh, you intend on keeping me in here, how nice."

"Be quiet Helga. Now we need a drink and talk this through." She hands me the gun and bullets and I hide them in the cupboard.

"What was those shots," she asks.

"Your guess is the same as mine." We are drinking our drinks and looking at the floor when there is a knock on my door. We look at each other as I get up and ask who is it, Roseburg says it's him. I open the door and he pushes in, when I look at him he has tears in his eyes. We both ask him what is the matter. I feel unsafe so the chair goes back under the door handle.

Roseburg starts to speak, "They have shot him dead."

"Who?" we ask.

"Stein, of course."

"But why?"

"He argued with Cristian tonight, something about what they wanted him to do, but he refused."

"What was it?"

"I don't know."

"We heard some shots fired, that must have been it, but where did they kill him?"

"Down stairs, in the warehouse. They will dispose of his body elsewhere. The suits did it."

"We will all have to be very careful from now on. Do you want a drink Roseburg?"

"No thanks, I must get back to my room." I move the chair and he leaves us with more to think about, which means, if you don't cooperate with them you are not worth being here.

"This is bigger than we thought," I say to Helga,

"We must toe the line till next week."

She leaves me and I get ready for bed. My head is in a whirl, I must think of some way of getting out of here and with Sonny's help blow this place up. We need a meeting soon then I fall asleep.

When I wake up, I think about last night. Get ready to go for the breakfast with Helga. We go into the dining room and see Cristian in there, already eating, he looks up and smiles, "Good Morning," he says. We both say morning to him as we sit down, and order some food. As I am drinking some coffee he says, "Oh by the way, Stein is not with us anymore, he had to leave in a hurry last night."

Yes, I think, *we know how.*

"So, you will be in the lab on your own but you will have a visit from Mr Wingers from time to time as he knows his way round your work and what we are doing here." I do not eat a lot; my stomach does not feel like it needs any food. "Off your food Rubin, you were shouting not long ago that the food was crap," Cristian said.

"No, I feel as if I have a tummy bug today but I am happy with the coffee, thank you." He gets up and leaves us. I don't see his two suits today with him, they must be disposing the body of stein.

Helga and I walk out of the dining room together. I say to her, "I would love to kill him first before we leave."

"Calm down Rubin. All in good time."

"Sorry but I am mad and need to calm down, let's get sorted to go in the lab and act as normal." We are now in the lab and I can't stop thinking about Stein, poor sod, he had a family who will not see him again and we could be next if we don't carry on with this project. Now shock horror, who comes in but Cristian, with Wingers from MIS, he says politely, "Hello, Rubin," and nods to Helga and Roseburg. His first words were, "How is it going? Will it be finished in time for the parade in Moscow?" Wingers is looking around and touching items.

I say, "I wish you would not touch things, please."

"Oh sorry," he says and looks at me with a smirk on his face. *You Bastard*, I think, *your time will come soon, you traitor*.

Cristian speaks, "Okay Rubin, no harm done. I can see you and your team have it all under control. If you need any more help for lifting or to get anything ask those men in white suits, you have my permission, and they have been told they are to help you for anything you need."

"Thank you Cristian." Then, they both start to leave but not before Wingers turns to me and gives me a creepy smile.

Roseburg comes close to me and whispers, "Meeting tonight in Helga's room. It's important, at 9:30." I just nod and we carry on working. We work through the day; the time goes fast and then I told them and the white suits to call it a day. We go through the getting out on to the lift and then, we go to our rooms.

"See you later, Helga," and I go into my room. As I turn the handle to open the door I look in with horror as I see Wingers sitting on my bed. Before I could say anything, he puts his finger to his lips and says, "Shut the door, Rubin. We need to talk. I only have a few minutes. I am not the bad guy you think I am; all will come out tonight at our meeting."

"What the bloody hell are you talking about?"

"Rubin, I am on your side, please, believe me! I will be at your meeting at 9:30, I have to go now, see you later okay?" I just nod as I feel dazed. I need a drink and get one and I sit down trying to put my head round it all.

After a shower and getting dressed, Helga knocks on my door and comes in. First thing she says is, "I am sure you were talking to someone earlier."

"Yes, I was and I will explain later. Let's go to dinner first." We go into the dining room and see that all the chairs are fully apart from two. So, we sit down, I look around and can see Cristian, next to Wingers, who looks at me and smiles. Plus, Roseburg, the two suits and one more person, it was a female, good looking and smiling at me.

Cristian says, "Let me introduce Professor Chinks. She will be helping you and your team, Rubin. She knows all about missiles and rockets and what you are making, so this will help to finish the dish on time."

I must admit the food has improved and the company. I can't help wondering when it's all going to end and when I could go home.

Everyone is pleasant at dinner and we finish on brandies, as Cristian likes us all drinking together. One by one, we get up and leave to go back to our rooms. As we are walking back, I say to Helga, "We are in your room for 9:30. Okay?"

"Yes."

"Alright, it's now 9:00 p.m., let's have a drink while we wait for the others."

"I need to put more slap on if I have all these men in my room."

"Oh, shut up, Helga. You pussy."

"Rubin I'll love it if you talk dirty to me."

"Stop it now, Helga. You're nuts."

While we are sitting in Helga's room, there is a gentle knock on the door. Then it opens and three people walk in, Roseburg, Sonny and Wingers.

"Hello!" I say and they smile and sit down. Helga asks if any one wishes for a drink but no takers.

"Okay, you start, as you called this meeting with Wingers in tow," Sonny speaks, "Don't be like that, Rubin. He can help us so I will ask him to tell us what he knows."

Wingers starts to talk first, "Yes, I know, it's a shock for you and Helga, but I work for MI5 and the USA plus Russia."

"So, you're a triple agent?" Helga butts in.

"Yes, sort of. While I am here, I will work with all of you to destroy this place and try and get us all out safe. Nothing here is as it appears, don't tuck Cristian off, he will terminate you just like Stein. Don't forget he sees everything and forgets nothing.

"The main man, Number '13', is a KGB boss who has set up shop inside the Kremlin. Russia is not the only major power to threat the other nations. MI5 did threat assessments and I am to believe that the conduct of China is equally alarming. China will have more economic power than the USA and it threatens us all. Russia's space programme is riddled with problems and there are way more Russians spies living in America with contacts all over the world."

"Plus, they have space parts being made in Albania."

"That's all well and good information," Rubin states, "We need to know what are the plans for getting out of here and blowing this bloody place up. I would like to get back to England."

Sonny butts in, "We all do, and we are working on a plan. Now you and Roseburg should finish the dish before the parade. I know that he is not releasing any of you until he comes back from the parade and if Number 13 is happy, you could end up staying to make more components."

"Fuck that," Rubin shouts.

"Keep quiet Rubin," Sonny says, "we don't want any suits here. Do we?"

"Sorry," he says, "Sonny, carry on."

"I listen to Cristian speaking on the phone so I know what the orders are for this place and as far as he is concerned it will stay open for business. So, keep calm and work properly and when you talk with him make it normal. Okay?!" Roseburg did not speak nor Helga. "When we meet again we will have a plan. So, don't worry any of you, we will have a helicopter when we leave, to take us to the airport."

"What about phones and passports?" Rubin whispers.

"I know where they are and will retrieve them for us. That and some other things are in his bunker, we need to get Cristian's finger prints to access the door code to get in the bunker."

"I agree, this is a dangerous place and we need to get out while we are still alive. We will meet in two days' time with the plan and with Rubin and Helga's input."

"Right, we better go. See you soon."

They leave.

"What a meeting that was, Rubin. Very heavy stuff."

"Yes, but all true. I need a drink. What about you?" Rubin makes the drinks and says, "Do you think we can trust those three?"

"What choice do we have?"

"True," Rubin nods his head. "I have an idea how to get those finger prints off Cristian, Helga. I will tell you later, I need a word tomorrow with the white suits in the lab."

"Now I am puzzled."

"Don't worry, it should work."

Helga is getting ready for bed so I wave to her as I start to leave her. "You can stay, Rubin."

"Not today, thank you. Bye," I leave, get back to my room and put the chair against the door handle then get ready for bed.

I wake up at about 5:00 a.m., no windows in our rooms so no idea what outside looks like. Coffee and shower, I feel good. Today I have a plan. Helga knocks on the door, "Are you ready? I can't get in."

"Coming!"

We go to breakfast and it's us and Roseburg. Just the three of us. We make some small talk and just keep a low profile in case we are being watched.

We finish our breakfast and head back to our rooms. We meet at the lift. "Here we go again," Helga says.

"Yes," Roseburg replies.

He seems very quiet, maybe fed up in here, same as us. We go through the routine, changing room, then glass tube, then doors into the lab. It's about 9:15 a.m. and I can see the white suits, well overall two of them. I go over to them and ask, "Did Cristian tell you that you two work for me now?"

They look at me and both say, "Yes."

Then one comments, "Is there anything wrong, or do you need something doing now?"

"Yes, I need some plastic bags and some cello tape to put the components in, so no dust gets into them. Okay?"

"Yes, sir."

I can tell from their accent they are not from the UK.

"Also, I will need some lifting to screw our dish together." Before they answer, I ask them "And what do you two do in here?"

"Well sir, we make these small electronic boards for your dish and for the missiles and rockets."

"Where do you eat and sleep?" I ask them.

"We have our own dormitory and next door to that is our dining room. We are on the second floor. There are other people in our room, sleeping, but we don't know where they work as they come and go at different times. The floor is empty as no one comes up there."

"Okay, thank you, carry on and I will call you when you are needed."

"Thank you, sir."

What! I thought. More people than I knew in this building. We can't blow it up with all them in here. I need to speak with them again. As I go back to my bench, Helga is looking at me with a face stare. I smile at her and whisper, "We have a problem. I'll tell you later. Get Roseburg."

When she does, he looks at me and says, "Okay, where are we at now on this dish?"

"Now I reckon we have about four days to get finished and have some sort of a plan in place. So, tonight I need to go on floor number two, find these white suits, talk to them and see if I can trust them."

"Okay, let's have a break, tell them two white suits, we will have coffee and a sandwich."

"What's going on, Rubin?" Helga asks me.

"We need to slow down so we have time on our side."

She nods with a smile. We ask the white suits to sit with us. I ask Helga to talk to them. "What about?" she says.

"Anything. Just keep smiling at them and talk at the same time. Can you do that?"

"Bitch," she calls me.

While she is talking, I move towards Roseburg and sit with him, we are slightly away from them. I say, "I need you to tell Sonny that we have more bodies to worry about and that I will be going to their room tonight to talk to them,"

"Be careful," he whispers.

I say loudly, "Yes that's right Roseburg, we will try it your way, he looks at me and scratch his head so he has the message." After a little more time wasted we go back to work. I ask Helga, "Did you learn anything from them?"

"Yes, I did Rubin."

We have had a good day at work and learnt things so we finish work and change and go back to our rooms. I shower and change and get ready to go to the dining room. Helga is outside and while we walk there, I say to her, "Just make sure you have a brandy after the meal."

"What?" she says.

"Just do it."

We walk in the room and look at the full table. Wingers looks at me with a smile and sitting near is Cristian, the two suits on his other side. Roseburg and Helga and me on the opposite side. The food smells good and it was. We are just talking when Cristian butts in and says to me, "How is the dish coming on, Rubin? I see you have got the white suits working for you now." God, he has eyes everywhere.

"Yes, they are very helpful and we are making progress with the dish."

Then he comments, "I need it finished in three days. Will it be done?"

"Yes, I think so."

Cristian doesn't think. "Rubin, I need it done, finished, okay?"

"Yes Cristian, we will have it done."

"Good, now who is up for brandy?" We all say yes and the two suits leave. We ponder over the brandies and Cristian and Wingers leave. I send Helga to the door and tell her to keep watch. She knows me by now and does not question what I say. Then, I get a plastic bag from my pocket, reach over the table and pick up Cristian's brandy glass with the plastic bag over my hand. I roll it over the glass then hide it under my jumper.

"Okay, let's go Roseburg." We make it back to my room while inside I hide the glass.

Helga asks me, "What are you doing? Have you gone mad?"

"All will be revealed in time. That glass is our ticket out of here."

"What did you learn from the white suits."

"I am not telling you until you get me a drink."

"Now who's the bitch? Here you are now, spill the beans."

"They both come from Romania. They got caught smuggling people and they have families back home. There were more of them but they were shot dead. These two were left alive as they had some electronics knowledge and they could work here. After some time, they would be released and flown back home but they fear for their lives and for their families."

"You did well, Helga. Now, tonight we are going to find them and have a further chat. They are on floor number two and we should disturbed anything when we go there."

"Did you think Roseburg was quiet today?"

"Yes. He did not speak to me unless I asked him something. I don't know why is he panicking about the plan or getting out. Let us hope he does not do anything stupid to cause any suspicion. We will go in a few minutes first. I am going to get the gun you found in Steins room." All I have ever done is clay shooting before, so a hand gun is different. I get the gun and hide in the back of my jeans. "You ready?

Let's go and don't say a word. Just follow me." We leave my room, go towards the stairs and follow them up to the second floor, not far away. As we creep along the walls to look for the room they are in, we get near the dining room and can hear voices. So, when I take a peek, I can see two people in there. So, I point to the floor and whisper, "Bend down and move fast." We get past and look for the dorm and see it opposite to us. I give a gentle knock and try the door, then turn the handle and we go in. We see our two white suits, only this time they are sitting at a table playing cards in normal clothes.

The two guys look at us staring, I speak first after shutting the door, "We need to talk with you both. What are your names?"

The dark-haired one says, "I'm Jann and he is called Mouse." Helga and I smiled.

"What sort of name is that," I say. "Okay don't bother." I guess it was because he was small. "You know our names, I need to ask you how long are you here for and if I can trust you well."

"We were told as long as they need us for," Jann says, "but we don't want to stay we want to leave, we don't like it here."

"Pleased to hear that. What about the other two in the dining room?"

"Same for them."

"Where do they work?"

"I think on the rocket or the missile. They don't talk much, they were thinking of getting out one night."

"Tell them to stay put for a while as that is what I came to see you about. We are going to try and leave in four days' time. Do you want to come as well?"

Jann says, "Yes," and Mouse nods his head.

"I am going to need everybody's help. Are you in for that?" they both nod. "You speak good English."

"Yes, we learnt it from moving people about."

"Okay we all carry on as normal and I will explain all the details to you later. I need you to talk to the other two and let me know what they say. Don't let me down." As I turn, they look at my gun in my jeans and that made it a bit more real to them I guess. "We must leave now; we'll talk later okay?" They look at us and seemed startled. We leave and sneak past the dining room and get back to my room safely. "Bloody hell Helga! What do you make of that?"

"Okay, yes, I know. Drinks first," she says.

"I think they are on our team, it's just the other two."

"Yes, if they are stupid they will get shot so, it is up to them."

"We have to come up with a plan for us and the others as soon as possible."

"Well, we have Jann and Mouse to help us," she giggles. "And I think Jann fancies me."

"Enough of that, we have to be serious now. Get to bed in your room."

"I love it when you are firm with me, Rubin."

"Good night, Helga."

She is gone and I try to think of how to get out. I need a plan of mine in case Sonny doesn't come up with one. I need another drink, then to bed. This all seems like a bad dream but the reality is that it's all bloody true and happening now. God, I need some sleep.

My alarm goes off and '*Bam*', and I go through my routine of coffee and shower. I don't know how Helga does it, she is in my room. I forgot to put the chair against the handle.

"Ready?"

"Yes, let's go."

We enter the dining room for breakfast and it is only us two. Something does not feel right, my stomach is feeling not so good. So, after a Spartan breakfast of espresso and dry toast, I am done. I nod to Helga so we then leave to get ready for work this time I can see suits everywhere on our walk back just standing about.

"Something is wrong I whisper to Helga."

"Let us just carry on Rubin, we don't know anything."

As soon as I get back to my room, I check to see if the gun was still where I hid it. Thank goodness it's still there. I just touch it and think, *I might have to use you.*

Helga and I go to the lift and do all the routine to get into the lab. More suits in the corridor before we get into the lift. When we arrive in the lab I see the two white suits working. Jann looks at me with a look of 'I need to talk'. I just nod to him and walk over as to talk about what they are working on. I point to the objects on their bench and move my arm about as if anyone is watching, they will think we are talking shop.

He starts to whisper and seems he is nearly crying. "The other two were caught last night trying to break out from here. I have not seen them since, we had some noise on our corridor but I dared not look outside my door. They must have been taken away." I did not know what to say.

"Okay it is too late for them so we carry on and I will contact you later." He nods with a distant face, thinking he won't get out alive. Don't worry, I will keep my word. We carry on working on our projects with my mind all over the place.

We work all day and finish up and get cleaned up ready for dinner. After dinner we are back in my room having drinks with Helga, chatting about the day and what happened last night. Helga says, "Think of them… poor families they have left behind Rubin."

"I am sorry for them; we did not know who they were."

Then Helga asks Rubin, "You are not married. Why? You are good looking and have a fit body and you have a girlfriend."

"We are more like friends with benefits. If I ever get married, it would be hard as when I see my male friends complaining about their marriage and how the sex is not so exciting, it makes me think.

"I would need a lovely girl who would bring up my children and look after the house but, she needs to be a whore in the bedroom. Then, I'll know that I have cracked it. But I don't know anyone who can say that. I know it works both ways, she would not have to work unless she wanted to. Maybe that's why many people stray and have affairs outside marriage."

"Oh Rubin, I never thought that of you. It has made me open my eyes about you. Anyhow don't try it on with the new professor, Miss Chinks, as she bats for the other side."

"Oh, I see. Well she has not been in my company yet, has she Helga?"

"You are so naughty, Rubin."

"We have more pressing matters to worry about than sex."

As I was pouring new drinks, I hear a tap at the door and Sonny and Wingers come in. "Yes, we will have one, please Rubin."

As I pass the drinks, Sonny says to us, "Have you heard about the two white suits? They tried to make a bolt out of here last night and were caught and taken away to be shot. I am telling you this so you are more careful in the future."

Rubin stands up and faces them, "We have six people to get out. Us four and the two white suits that work with me."

"Bloody hell Rubin, that's too many to worry about," Sonny says.

"I made a promise to them for helping me so its seven or none. Anyhow, I hold a trump card up my sleeve over the last few days. I have taken Cristian's brandy glass away."

"So what?" Wingers butts in.

"Hang on, I will explain. Now I have the glass and what you will do Sonny is with this cello tape, take his finger prints off the glass. So, with his prints we will be able to get in his bunker and set the rocket off to explode after we leave. What do you think, can you do it Sonny?"

"Great idea, Rubin. I will put it all together. Let's hope his finger prints are the same as the rocket and bunker needs."

"What do you mean?"

"Sometimes people have new skin pieces put on their fingers for such a time."

Wingers joins in with, "The UK knows of this place as I have informed them and they want it destroyed. They can't do anything to raise suspicion so they are hoping we can pull it off. Now on the day of the parade, we will leave when not many suits are around. I will work out time and place to meet. Is that understood by everyone here?"

"Yes!" we all say.

"Where is Roseburg?"

"He, the KGB and Cristian have a meeting about the parade times etc. I don't think he will be with us as he has to go with Cristian to the parade."

"Poor sod."

So now we have six people to worry about. Sonny and Wingers get up and leave us. "Right Helga, it is on in two days, that's it."

"Hopefully! What a day! Too much information, Rubin, for me."

"With a bit of luck, we will get out of here with what we came in with, Helga."

"And what is that, Rubin? Nothing! No money, nothing!"

So, it is late and I need some sleep. When my alarm goes off in the morning, I do my coffee and shower and Helga comes in. I am not dressed yet so I shout, "You are an early bird today."

"I could not sleep, Rubin," she talks while I dress. I think she comes in early to catch me with no clothes, on purpose. "Take your time Rubin."

"Oh, shut up you, okay. Let's go for the breakfast." As we walk our way it seems to be quiet today; no one around, and when we are in the room, no one but us two again. So, it's coffee and toast. Helga has muesli and then we leave for our rooms to get ready once again. Then into the lift and off we go, finally we get into the lab and the white suits are waiting for us to start on the dish. No sooner had we got there when Miss Chinks shows up and says, "Good morning! Cristian sent me to check on your progress." *God, she is lovely! What a shame she is not straight*, I thought. I could see the white suits looking at her contently and waiting for every word she says.

"Rubin!" she calls. "How far have you got with this dish? As I understand you will be making several of these for us." If that's what she thinks, I will say nothing.

"Yes, we have a good day to finish it. Should be some time tomorrow for you to take it away." Miss Chinks looks at me in straight in the eyes, thanks me and asks what are their roles here, pointing to the suits. "They make the components for this dish under my instructions." I reply.

"Very good, keep busy. I will see you later. Bye," and she leaves by the other side of the lab. I see Jann looking at me and he comes over.

I whisper to him, "On parade day, we are off okay?"

His reply was, "We did some looking around and past our rooms. There is another corridor that goes the length of the building with a door at the end, which I think goes out onto the roof."

"Good man! That might help us. Now carry on working and I will keep you informed." Off they go, singing some tune which I had never heard before.

So now, Roseburg comes in to help and says to me, "Cristian thinks something is going on and his suits have been told to tighten up the security and I have to go with the boss and the KGB to the parade so I am stuck here."

"Maybe not here old boy, somewhere else or home who knows. eh?"

Roseburg says, "I hope my country will get me out as I work for the secret intelligence service of the state of Israel."

"Wow, you are a dark horse, Roseburg. I don't know who you work for anymore in here."

"Don't worry Rubin, your secrets are safe with me and you will be out soon."

"I hope so," I whisper.

"My plan is to slip away from the parade as my agents will be there to help me. I thought I had blown it when I used my mobile near your rooms instead of mine. I did not know that it got picked up here by the overhead satellite. That's why the suits came and searched your rooms. That time do you remember?"

"Yes, I do, I had forgotten about it."

"So, what are your plans Rubin?"

I then thought before I answered, "No nothing yet, it seems hard in this place as you are being watched all the time." I don't know if I can trust him as he is up Cristian's arse. So, I tell him nothing and carry on working and checking the suits' work to make sure it's compatible. When I see Helga looking at me, I slide my hand across my neck so as to signal her to say nothing to Roseburg. She just nods back. The suits seem to be in good spirits and are smile when I talk to them to check all the diagrams and tell them we need to finish this by tomorrow.

"No problem, Rubin. We will have it all done for you." Now I remember that I had made a slight change to the dish in its circumference so it should not direct anything properly, I hope. We work and after a while take a break as to waste time. I let the suits sit on their own and us three sit together.

I say to Roseburg, "Not seen you for breakfast for a while now."

"I have mine with Cristian because he said I have to be with him in the mornings so as to find out what the day has in store."

"Did you know that two of the white suits are missing?"

"No!" he said. Now I know he is lying and I cannot trust him. I need to tell Sonny and Wingers as they might give our plans away.

It comes to late afternoon and I have had enough of work so I tell the suits to knock it off. Helga and I get changed, leave and get back to our rooms. I lay on my bed thinking about Roseburg, *what's he up to*, I wonder. Who else can I not trust? At least I have Helga on my side with only a day to go. As I am laying there I hear a small scuffle, then a piece of paper comes under the door, I retrieve it and look at it. *Meeting tonight in your room, 9:30*, no name on it. Could it be a double cross from Roseburg who might have put it under my door? So, is this is it now a plan to be hatched to get us chickens out of here for real?

Who knows? no good thinking about it now. So, I get ready for dinner and this time I knock on Helga's door. "Come in, I am not dressed yet, whoever you are." When I open the door and go in, Helga is smiling,

"Hello Rubin!"

"You are dressed."

"Yes, but you did not know that and wanted to see me in my undies."

"Leave it out, you are just a wind up, Helga."

"Yes, but you love me for real."

"No comments," I say, "come on, let's go to dinner." When we arrive, the table is full except for our two seats. Cristian, Wingers, the professor, two suits and a face I have not seen before. Cristian says, "Good evening to you two. Let me introduce this gentleman—the one I don't recognise—I will just say he works for the KGB. He would like a tour round your lab Rubin. Do you think you would do that for me after dinner?"

Shit what about our meeting! He must be Number 13. As I am thinking, I hear out loud, "Rubin, is that alright?"

"Yes, sorry, I was thinking of dinner."

"Okay. Let's hope it's good tonight Rubin. It should keep you happy." *Yeh, Yeh Cristian*, I thought to myself.

"Yes, and it was a good choice of duck steak. You name it, was on the menu." This must have been said showing off to Number 13 that we eat well. *Make the most of it, this could be your last dinner, who knows?* Everyone was talking, mainly the professor to Number 13 like she had known him from before. I need to eat quickly and get finished as I have to show Number 13 around the lab. I nod to Helga and gesture to eat up. I say our excuses and ask to leave and thank Cristian for his hospitality. "No brandy Rubin?"

"Not tonight. I think I should better have a clear head."

"Good man," he says.

We are about to leave when I turn around and say to Number 13, "I will meet you near the lift in 30 minutes. Is that alright for you?"

He nods and says, "Yes, thank you, Rubin."

We leave and get back to my room. Helga looks at me, "You are cutting it fine, with our meeting for 9:30."

"Well, you will have to start without me. You can bring me up to speed later if I miss anything."

"Rubin, you know I am no good without you by my side."

"Don't worry, I will protect you at all times from now on."

"Thank you," she whispers and kiss her lips with her finger and place it on my mouth. Then not another word, she leaves me. If she was real, I could love her too. Well here I am at the lift, waiting, when I hear some footsteps, then I see Number 13 with two of his heavies. *Can't trust me or anyone, I guess. Mean looking dudes.* As one of them moved his jacket, I could see his gun in a holster.

We go into the lift and into the room and I tell him he will have to put on the overalls and point to them for his heavies as well. We are in the chamber and go into the lab. "Now, show me what you are working on Rubin." I take him to the dish, he looks at it and says, "It's not finished yet." *Does he have knowledge of these things or is he bluffing me?* "Who works on this bench Rubin?"

"There are two men who work on the components for the dish."

"I can see you are well set up and for your next dish. I understand it will be bigger than this one as this a prototype."

I just say, "Yes." What the hell? He doesn't know what I have planned.

"Is there anything else I should see?"

"No sir, this is all we are working on."

"Good. I think this lab will do fine—the size and equipment for future dishes and missiles. I say, shall we go then?" As I sneak a look at the time, *9:25!* We turn to leave when he says to me, "You are happy here then, Rubin?"

"Yes, thank you. Although it would be good to have some fresh air or seeing my family."

"I will see what I can do for you, Rubin." Too late now for kindness. *What about the people who have been shot?* I think, and say, "Thank you that would be nice."

Then we get to go out the same way. As we leave the lift onto the corridor, he says, "Would you like to come and have a chat and a drink with me Rubin?"

"May I take a rain check?"

"Maybe some other time then," he says. As I say bye to him and go to my room, I find there Sonny, Helga and Wingers. It is now 9:40.

"Not too late, Rubin."

"No, but I need a drink. I don't know what he is planning in his head but he thinks we are all here for good. I did not think he would leave me, he said something about expanding this plaice for more missiles and dishes and then he wants me to have a drink with him."

"He must like you," Sonny chips in.

"Okay, let's see what we are doing tomorrow night."

Wingers starts with, "Cristian is leaving tonight late and has asked me to go, so I said I will see him there."

"What have you got, Sonny?"

"Tonight, later on when it's my shift, I will go into Cristian's room and try to get into the bunker with the finger prints you gave me. I have transferred them onto some rubber gloves which I will put on. Now there is a time lock of ten minutes so I don't know until then if they will work. Also, there will be about three suits left in the building to look after us. I need to get in to retrieve a phone to call up a chopper. I cannot use these land lines as they are monitored.

"I suggest we try and leave at 6:00 p.m. So, you need to tell your white suits Rubin."

Rubin butts in, "Look, you must not say anything to Roseburg as he is on Cristian's side. I think we should meet at the lift and then way up on the roof. If we go to the suits' corridor, there is a door to the roof past their dorm. You must be able to have that helicopter on the roof at 6:00 p.m. sharp."

Wingers starts talking, "Yes we know about Roseburg as we put him to the test (he saw the bait but not the hook). He has been spending too much time with Cristian, we noticed, so now it is just us six to go."

Sonny starts with, "I have a gun and I will see if I can find more of them—I decided that I was not going to mention my gun. We found in Stein's room—and some hand grenades to put under the rocket and in the lab. Once it blows, it will catch fire, then the building will blow with all the explosives in it."

Helga butts in, "I don't know much about bombs but I know that a grenade will blow in seconds. How will you get away from that in time?"

"Not these ones, they have a timer attached to them. I don't know, technically, much about all the systems in here, including the bomb shelter. All we have to worry about is the other three suits walking about checking everywhere. Besides, can you trust the other two white suits, Rubin?"

"They were up for getting out and I think we can trust them."

"It seemed that it must have been one of the other two white suits that disappeared that used a phone as it was tracked by an overhead-NSA-spy-satellite, floating high in the sky. Big brother watches us and listens to us as well."

"Right back to us, we get picked up and go straight to the airport on the USA camp about 100 miles away. Then, flown to the UK and another plane for you Helga to go back to America. Have we all got that."

"What about you Sonny?"

"I shall stay on the camp to debrief the Federal Secret Service. You, Rubin and Wingers, will be in the UK and you two will debrief the MIS and MIG at the GCHO. When it comes to it, they will let you know, Rubin, as Wingers will be there from here. We hope all of us get out in one piece and you, Helga, will be met of your plane and taken to talk to some secret agents. Is everyone clear now?"

"I have to get passports and phones out of the bunker tonight after Cristian has left with the KGB guy with some of their heavies, so leave that to me. Has anyone got anything more to say?"

Winger starts to say, "I have to hide tomorrow so no one see me as Cristian will be waiting for me and no doubt he will ring the heavies to see if I have left for the parade or not."

Rubin says, "And we go into the lab as usual and tell the white suits what's going on. Right, its late so we better leave, see you tomorrow at 6:00 p.m. Bye."

Wingers and Sonny leave us, I ask Helga, "Want a drink?"

"Yes, please Rubin. I feel very nervous about all this."

"Helga, you will stick to me like glue. I will not let anything happen to you. You mean a lot to me and I will keep my promise about your operation."

"Thank you, Rubin. You mean a lot to me too and I need you more than ever. If only things were different."

"Yes, I know what you mean and I agree. Once I get out of here and have some down time, I will be over to the States for business and I will see you then."

"You promise, Rubin?"

"Yes, I have given you my private number. So, ring me to tell when you are safe. Now stop all this and have another drink, then you can go to your room."

"Can I stay with you tonight, Rubin? It is our last night and I feel safer when I am with you."

"Okay." *What am I saying?* "No playing around, I will sleep on the settee and you can have the bed."

"I will smell your body that will make me sleep soundly."

"Better than me, no doubt." After a bit more idle chit-chat we got ready to sleep.

I did not sleep too badly, better than I thought. Helga was still asleep, so I woke her up with a coffee. "I slept good, Rubin. Thank you. I feel better this morning."

"I will go so we can get ready for breakfast. See you soon." She leaves and then I shower and change into some casual clothes.

Helga and I go to breakfast as normal, toast and lots of coffee for me, and muesli for Helga with orange juice. No one else is in here, it seems quiet.

We don't stay long and head back to our rooms by 9:00 a.m. We both get to the lift and outside the lift is one of the heavies with an automatic machine gun. We say morning to him and he just grunts something back so we smiled. We get into the lift and carry on with our ritual of getting ready for the lab.

Getting there, I see the two white suits and Jann looks at me. (I'm thinking these boys must start earlier than us) I go over to Jann and whisper, "It's on for tonight. Meet us at the fifth floor at 6:00. Use the stairs to that level, not the lift, but before you come, check if we can get to the corridor that leads to the roof, okay?" They both hear me and just stare. *What now? Have they changed their minds?* I think. Then they smile and just nod their heads to acknowledge what I just said to them. I walk away and talk loud saying, "…and I want that component finished by 2:00 p.m."

They reply, "Yes, Rubin."

As I get back to my bench I look up, and to my surprise, I see that Miss Chinks has arrived in the lab. *What is she doing here*, I think. *She should be at the parade. Is this going to mess our plans up?* She comes over to me ignoring Helga with, "Hello Rubin." She is holding some papers and smiles at me. Then she says, "How is the dish coming, will it be finished today?"

"Yes, Miss Chinks, by about 4:00 p.m."

"Oh good, I shall call Cristian and tell him. Now I have a plan here for your next dish. This will be four times bigger than this one. We will be drafting in more people to help on this one. I want you to keep these plans to study. Any questions?"

"No."

"Good, I shall now go to the parade where I am expected. It starts at 2:00 p.m. and goes on for about 4 to 5 hours, depending on the weather; if the president stays." She says nothing to Helga. Only gives her a look that could kill, she must know about Helga and disapprove.

We carry on working, I want this finished and put to bed by 4:00 p.m. Knowing that I cut the dish at the wrong angle of the diameter to the dish, after having to get on working faster and putting it all together with help of Jann, I stand back with a sigh of relief and say, "Okay, let's go. It's now 4:05. Get cleaned up." So, Helga and I go our way. I never did find out the other route out which the white suits take. We get out of the lift and no one is around this time, can't hear anything.

We go into my room and sit down when Helga says, "Who the bloody hell does she think she is? That Miss Chinks stuck-up bitch, I find her unbearably rude, Rubin. No chinks in her armour there. I heard she works for the Secret Federal Services in Russia.

"She also has a post in the state-run pharmaceutical company in Serbia. Someone needs to stop her. She is dangerous."

"Russia has its fingers in a lot of countries. Spies. Do you know Helga? Even if we did blow this place up, no doubt they will build another one somewhere? These plans will be coming to me to the UK to be handed in. I am not going to give them to Wingers. He might sell them to the highest bidder."

"Why don't you Rubin, or keep them for you to build at your own factory?"

"Helga (I love you) I never thought of that. Yes, it is in my programme of work. I might, we will see."

"Rubin, I need to ask you something. When, or if we get out of here, I want to fly with you to the UK and stay with you till I feel safe to travel back to America."

"You want to stay with me at my home for a while?" *Yes please. Oh God, what am I getting into?* "What about Sonia, my girlfriend?"

"Well she knows you're safe with me."

"I don't think so you can twist me round your little finger."

"I know."

"It's good, okay. We will try, you will have to be debriefed in the UK first I guess."

"Thank you, Rubin," and then she gets up from her seat and goes to Rubin and kisses him on the cheek. "You are so sweet, that Sonia does not deserve you."

"I think you are trouble sometimes. You now need to get ready and put on some warm clothes and flat shoes, not high heels. No dressing up, this is not the time, and I want you back here by 5:30 p.m."

"Okay, Rubin, whatever you say. You are in charge." She leaves I start to get ready and look for the gun we found in Steins' room. I stick it in the back of my jeans hoping it won't be noticed, but really, I don't care. If it helps us out then that's all care about. 5:20, Helga comes back in jumper and trousers and flat shoes, but still with face make-up on. She still looks good even like that.

"Rubin my hands are shaking and I am nervous as hell."

"If it helps, so am I. No drinks. We need a clear head."

Just then a faint knock on the door and Sonny comes in with a large bag over his shoulder. Rubin says to Sonny, "We should all meet at the lift, then down the stairs to floor two and along the corridor to where the stairs are to the roof."

Then Sonny speaks, "You two alright?"

"Yes, we are okay. Where's Wingers?"

"He will be here; he has been hiding all day."

"Did you get the passports and phones."

"Yes, and some extra bits like document and some explosives, it was tough getting in. I had transferred the finger prints on to rubber gloves it was not straight forward it took 25 minutes to get in as the prints on the panel show green when it's the correct one. What I did not know was you had to use both sets to activate all the lights green, then a click on the door and I was in. It took a while, I could not take everything, as it would have been too much to carry, so I have two small hand guns and grenades with a trigger. I spent too long in there as the time lock was shutting the door, but I did not leave without leaving a present for him, which should go off about 6:20 pm in the bunker and destroy things in there."

Next, a knock on the door and Wingers comes in. Sonny speaks again, "This is the plan, I will go first and leave some grenades in the rocket room now. They have a trigger with a timer, which looks like a mouse trap. The pin pops out and *bang*! And also, I will put three in the lift and send it down to the lab, but not until we are on the move as when the lift blows the heavies will come running.

"The heavies will be on this floor at 6:15 so we need to move fast. I am sending the lift down to the lab when I leave that floor. When the lift moves, the cameras will show this floor, at present they are showing the parade."

Wingers says, "I have a gun."

"Okay, we will be the last to leave, you can keep watch while I put the grenades in place." Sonny keeps talking, "I have ordered the helicopter for 6:05. If it come any earlier, it will be heard and checked on their radar. It should fly under the radar, otherwise they might send jet fighters up which we don't need. When you get to the base, an aeroplane will be waiting to go and one for you Helga…"

Rubin jumps in, "She is coming to the UK and coming with me to stay at my place for a while."

"Okay, one more thing. We have to shoot to kill because if they see us trying to leave, they will shoot us. Now, I hope none of you have said anything to anyone else."

"I have told the two who are coming with us."

Helga says, "No, not told anyone. This is like you read about in books." We all look at her and smile.

Meanwhile, Cristian is still at the parade. It's nearly finished. He is seated near Roseburg, Miss Chinks, the KGB's Number 13, the heavies and on his other side is the President smiling and waving. Cristian turns to Roseburg and says, "Where is Wingers? He should be here. Find out where he is, I am concerned. Go, then let me know."

After a while Roseburg comes back and says, "He left this morning as no one has seen him."

"Right, send some of the men back to find out."

Rubin asks Sonny, "Is anyone left in the building now?"

"No, only us and a handful of suits. Little do they know the place will be smarming soon with suits. I have some important documents which will help the USA to combat any of this planning to abuse other countries."

"Right, does anyone need a pit stop?"

"What's that?" Helga says.

"Toilet," Rubin says.

"Yes, I do."

"It is now 5:55 p.m. Wingers and I will go to start, and don't forget Wingers, 'Shoot to kill'." He nods and checks his gun. Sonny leaves with Wingers. We have a few minutes, Helga sticks with me.

"I will keep you safe."

"I trust you, Rubin."

"Right, it's our time now. Let's go." He grabs Helga's hand and leaves his room.

We start to walk to the lift like we have done many times but this time it's different. We don't need the lift, when we approach it, the two suits are there. Jann and Mouse are waiting. "Good to see you boys, let's get down those stairs to the roof." So off we go, it is some distance to these stairs.

When Mouse starts to go up, he shouts back, "It has a padlock on the hatch, I cannot open it." So, I climb up and see, it is not moving. I think there is only one way and that is to use my gun to shoot it off. I pull my gun from the back of me and then they freeze thinking it is some kind of a trick.

I say, "Don't worry, I am going to shoot the padlock." Relief all round. So, I fired a shot at it and it sprung away and Mouse went up and pushed on the trap door.

"I still can't move it."

God, my heart is thumping, my adrenalin is flying, and I say, "Get out of the way," and run up the stairs, and with my hands and head I jumped up at the trapdoor and, to my surprise, it flew open and we could see the sky. "Everyone, up, up now and quick. Stay on the roof and watch for the chopper. I am going back to see where the other two are." My head hurts, but I go back and, on the way, I hear shooting. "Shit!" They must have heard when I shot the padlock off. As I turn the corner, I see Wingers bending and looking at two suits who are firing at him. So, I get behind and ask, "Where's Sonny?"

"He is stuck in the lift, the door shut before he got out and then there was a shot from somewhere, and these goons came running. Okay, I will see if I can get near the lift and shout to Sonny."

I take the lift down to the second floor then send it down to the lab. The shooting stops so I lay on my tummy towards the lift, when I shout to Sonny, "What to do then, crawl back to Wingers?"

While we are there behind us a voice says, "What are you doing?" We turn around and Sonny is facing us.

"Come on," he shouts "We have to go, everything will go off and we are late for the chopper. I will stay here while you two go. I will follow after I have shot a few rounds off to hold them. Now go." Wingers and myself are up the stairs and the chopper is there, very noisy. We get in and it is only a minute but it seems a long time waiting. Even in the chopper, we could hear shots being fired.

"Give me your gun, Wingers. I am helping Sonny." As I get to go down the stairs, I see Sonny trying to climb them but he is struggling. Looks like he has been shot. So, I put my hand down and tell him to grab hold. As I lean down, I can see two suits chasing down the corridor, shooting at the hatch, so I fire-off Wingers gun and hit one in the leg as I still try to pull Sonny up. "Come on man, get up here." His top half comes through and then his legs. All I see is blood everywhere. I stand up and try to lift him and shout to Wingers to help us. Then Helga comes out of the chopper and helps to put Sonny into the chopper. I turn back and slam the hatch down as there were men climbing up the stairs so I fired into the hatch several times and then turned to get in the chopper. Helga is still standing waiting for me; I shout over the noise and we climb in and it lifts off. Just then some suits come out of the hatch and start firing at us; the bullets hit the chopper and one found Helga's foot. As we climb in, I then saw a serviceman at the doorway, on a big machine gun, firing at the suits as we are lifting off and it looks like he got a few kills.

We are in the air so I look at Helga who is crying. Her foot is bleeding bad. Then I look at Sonny who has been shot in the chest and lying down, with a man giving him some morphine to ease the pain. Jann and Mouse are in the corner and Wingers is asking how long this will take. Then we all rolled over as the chopper turned abruptly. "What the hell?" Wingers said. "I only ask how long will it take." We all laughed.

The pilot shouted, "That was a missile attack." They are playing dirty down there. When I looked out, I saw loads of cars with people running around, they must have come back from the parade. We are now out of sight and we hear a voice shout, "About 30 minutes to base," and they are on alert for action.

I try to comfort Helga. She says, "I won't be able to dance now, Rubin or get my heels on, it hurts like mad."

"I am sorry for you but Sonny is in a bad condition."

We are flying low over properties and can see the roofs. "We have ten minutes," a voice shouts, "Keep your fingers crossed and anything else."

We all look at each other. I think I can hear Jann and Mouse praying. I look at them and say, "Do one for Sonny and Helga."

She looks at me and says, "I love you Mr Johnson."

The pilot shouts, "We are two minutes away, but I can see a light in the sky, heading our way. We need to be over our air space to be safe." Then a shout comes from him, "Heads down!" and a loud noise goes over the chopper. The pilot shouts, "We have been hit, but we are there, so it might be bumpy." We finally land with our hearts in our mouths. We can't believe we are here. Then I see an ambulance coming towards us, the paramedics come in for Helga and Sonny, they take them away.

Helga is shouting to me, "Rubin I need you with me."

"I'm coming," I shout back and she is gone. I say to Wingers, "I am not getting on that plane until I know Sonny is safe and Helga is sorted."

"I agree Rubin."

Then Jann says, "What do we do now?"

"Come inside and you will be debriefed and then on a flight home, and don't get caught again."

They come over to me and shake my hand and say, "Thank you friend. We owe you our lives. If you are ever in our country, look us up, we will look after you. Thank you again."

They are taken away and both turn and wave to me. I wave back, then proceed to the building, but not before I go to the pilot and shake his hand and thank him for putting his own life in danger along with his co-pilots.

"All in a day's work, we do this all the time, but you don't read about it."

When I go in the building, I ask a staff member and say, "Where are my friends gone? They were injured." She points the way. When I go into the room, Wingers is already there so I ask him. Sonny is being operated on now and Helga is having the bullet removed. She has no bones broken. We drink coffee for about an hour and then the door opens and I see Helga on crutches coming towards me. She flings her arms around me dropping the crutches to the floor, she has tears in her eyes and hugs me hard. "Okay baby, calm down now. You are safe." When I look at her feet I see she has a moon boot on her foot. I bend down and pick her crutches up and laugh at her, "God, woman, you frighten me sometimes."

After about 30 minutes, a surgeon comes through to us and says, "Sonny is safe. The bullet missed his heart. He was lucky, someone was looking after him and praying I think."

"You don't know how true that is. Can we see him?"

"Yes, only five minutes. He's groggy, but go in."

When I see Sonny, he has tubes attached to him and a heart monitor. When he sees us, he smiles and grabs my arm and whispers, "Thank you Rubin, you saved my life. I will never forget that. I owe you." I was in shock. Wingers was saying something to him but I was still thinking he is alive. We all got out. Thank you, God!

A nurse comes in, "That's enough, thank you. You are all wanted by security near the main entrance." So, we leave and wave him good bye.

At security, we are told our plane is ready to fly to the UK, "You have five minutes. You will be directed when you leave with this man on your plane. Thank you for your help."

We get on a buggy and it takes us to a plane. Not too big for a plane, looks more like an executive jet. I help Helga up the stairs and we find two seats together. I settle her down, when a lady asks us, "Would you like a drink?"

"Yes please. Two large vodka and tonics please." She returns with the drinks and a tray of nibbles which are put on a table in front of us. Helga drinks her drink then puts her head on my shoulder and falls asleep. I think, *never mind the security for debrief. What about Sonia?* Then I doze off.

We are woken by, "We are landing now." That was quick. We land on the tarmac and taxi to a spot miles from the terminal.

We stop and the doors open. Two black suits come in and walk up to me and say, "Hello, Mr Johnson. Would you come with us please?"

I say, "Well my friend here needs some help getting off."

"No problem, sir," and he is on his wrist, talking to someone.

Next, more suits come on to help Helga. I say, "What about you, Wingers?"

"I have to go straight to the headquarters. I have to get off as I have a car waiting for me." Helga and I get into a smart car. We are seated at the back with TV and a drinks cabinet.

In the front, next to the driver, a head turns and says, "Well done Rubin."

"I never did anything. It was Sonny and Wingers who saved us."

"No, you saved Sonny I hear and Wingers is singing your praises." I am gob smacked. I am speechless and just look at this person. "Sorry," he says, "Let me introduce myself. I am Jones, head of security for the UK and we are off to our headquarters for your debrief in London. You will be well looked after. You are both booked into the Hilton and our car will pick you up at 9:00 a.m."

"We are at the hotel and we have no clothes."

"Don't worry, it's all taken care of. They're in your rooms. We are dropped off." I still have a weird feeling about this with cars picking me up.

"Can your person have a code word when they come please, as this has happened before?"

"What would you like? You choose."

"Okay, its 'Rubber'. That's what your driver will ring and say on our room phone. Okay?"

"Yes, Mr Johnson. 'Rubber' it is. Bye for now."

We go up to our rooms, both next to each other but with connecting internal doors. I say to Helga, "Don't forget to take your moon boots off before you get into bed." She puts her tongue out at me and disappears. "See you in the morning Helga," I shout.

The rooms were great and, yes, some clothes for me, all new from Marks. *They must have an account there*, I thought. I am tired so I get into bed and sleep, but I think, *why did they not want us straight away for debrief?* In the morning there is a knock at the door and next I have a breakfast fit for a king brought in on a trolley. "Would Sir like me to prepare it?"

"No thanks, I can manage." They leave.

Next the internal door opens and Helga is hobbling in and says, "Have you seen this much food? I have the same. We will share yours," and we do. Then we get ready and wait for the call to say the car is here. The phone rings.

"Hello. Is that Mr Johnson?"

"Why?"

"Rubber." The phone stays silent. "We are waiting at the main entrance."

"I will be down soon." Now we go down the stairs and it was hard work for Helga with her moon boots. I have a thing about lifts. We are downstairs. I wait a minute and look around, then at the door I see a man in a suit and walk towards him.

He looks at me and says, "This way please," and walks to the car and opens the door. I am helping Helga as she has left the crutches behind and pushes herself in first. She screams out loud and I look in and see none other than Roseburg sitting there.

"Morning to you," he says slowly.

What the hell is happening now? Are we being kidnaped and back to Russia? I am still holding Helga and she is clutching my arm tight. And I am confused in this.

"Why were we put in the hotel? Is this a double bluff? We are in our own country. Something is wrong here. What is it Roseburg? Tell me," I am shouting while the car is travelling; to which place? I don't know. Is this why Wingers did not come with us? The next minute my head is spinning. Next I fall and all the lights go out. It seems forever, I cannot focus or hear properly. We are moving I know that.

"Rubin, Rubin," I can hear my name being called. As I come round, slowly I feel that I am strapped to a chair. "Rubin," then my face is being moved and I wake up and can hear noises.

"Where are we?" Then I look and see Helga sitting near me and then see we are on a plane.

"Oh, fuck! No, not back there to Russia."

"Listen, silly, we are on our way to Scotland for a debrief. That's why it was not done last night."

"But I saw Roseburg in the car, didn't I?" Then I look around the plane and see Mr Jones who smiles at me and some other people. I think I feel a bit safe. "Why did I pass out then?"

"They gave you a quick jab to quiet you down as you were causing too much attention outside the Hilton."

Mr Jones comes over, "Morning, Rubin."

"Never mind about the morning. What the bloody hell is going on?"

"We are on our way to Scotland to one of our buildings. We needed to get you away as we had a tip-off that you were high on a kill list from Russia. So here we are, flying."

"Why am I in trouble?"

"Well Rubin, on the grapevine we heard of a factory going up in smoke and lots of loud bangs. Do you know anything about this?"

"Maybe," I said.

"Well Russia did not put it on the news. It had a black out on it. But I can tell you, we are very pleased with your efforts."

"It was not all me. Helga helped and Wingers. Oh, how's Sonny?"

"He sends you his regards and said you saved his life."

"Well, it is one place we don't have to worry about again. We have your plans and documents from Sonny which are of great importance to us.

"When we get off after we have had a chat with you both, we will fly you back to the nearest airport and take home."

"Okay I am not going nuts. I saw Roseburg in that car, didn't I?"

"Yes and no. We needed someone who recognised you at the hotel; he does work for us."

"What? I can't believe it! Who is straight in this country?"

"We try and keep our fingers on the pulse Rubin, to keep all in check. But he was at the parade. Yes, and when Cristian sent him back with your heavies, as you call them, he then flew here to fill us in on what he knew of your plans, but had to show a big front to Cristian that he was loyal."

"I don't like him."

"In our job, we don't like a lot of people but we work with them."

We touch down and are picked up and taken inside a big building into a room and I ask Mr Jones, "Did the other two get home alright?"

"I was hoping you would not ask but it saddens me totally when they arrived home they were ambushed and one got killed. I think he is called Mouse. Does that mean anything to you?" Helga holds my arm tight all this time. She has said nothing. "We think, by the time Cristian found out about your plan, he put the wheels in motion and as there are a lot of Russians in London. That's why we moved you. We found out this morning, as he told Roseburg, not knowing he came to the UK this morning."

"You seem to know a lot about what is going on."

"Yes, we have to be one step ahead of the others. Shall we start then? You can go." After about four hours, we were done and on our way home, but I am told we have to go to a safehouse first and you will have a body guard with you. We land and then get taken to some place in the country.

God, I will have some explaining to do to Sonia and work. No one will believe me. I ask Helga, "We need to get you booked in for your operation as soon as it's okay, and I think it will be best if you change your name. Can you think of one?"

"Yes, I can. Mrs Johnson." I collapse down with laughter.